Walter Stephens

Blackfriars

Or, the monks of old. A romantic chronicle. Vol. 2

Walter Stephens

Blackfriars
Or, the monks of old. A romantic chronicle. Vol. 2

ISBN/EAN: 9783337252298

Printed in Europe, USA, Canada, Australia, Japan

Cover: Foto ©Andreas Hilbeck / pixelio.de

More available books at **www.hansebooks.com**

BLACKFRIARS;

OR,

THE MONKS OF OLD.

A Romantic Chronicle,

IN THREE VOLUMES.

VOL. II.

LONDON:

LONGMAN, GREEN, LONGMAN, ROBERTS & GREEN.

1864.

LONDON:
RICHARD BARRETT, PRINTER,
MARK LANE.

BLACKFRIARS;

OR,

THE MONKS OF OLD.

CHAPTER I.

The Hospice in the Wilderness.

WE must now introduce our readers to the tavern of the "Three Bells," a place of entertainment for man and beast, somewhat famed at the period whereof we write. Perched directly beneath the high walls enclosing the monastic precincts on the eastern side, and close adjoining the river's bank, stood this well-known place of public festal resort. It was a large, substantial-looking erection of the good old style. Facing a broad wharf, against which the waters lashed and fumed each ebb and flow, it presented an enclosure surrounded on three sides by the buildings and adjuncts forming the requisites for an efficient and first-class house of public resort, while the fourth side was occupied by a grass plot, in the centre whereof stood a patriarchal oak of noble dimensions, beneath whose broad shadow were ranged manifold tables and benches. The inns of those days were very different structures to the meagre, compact ones of modern times ; and, as the " Three Bells" was the only recognised tavern within the precincts, it was, as may be imagined, a very extensive building. It stood upon the site of an ancient fortalice, that at one time had numerous mazy windings and secret entrances, and part whereof, in the form of a single turret, called *Camera Dianæ*, or Diana's Chamber, still stood adjoining the hostel at the back.

* Vide Appendix, Note 7.

Each story projected so much beyond the lower, that this ancient building, crowned with its fanciful gables and heavy chimneys, looked for all the world top-heavy, and as if it would roll down and pitch headlong some day into the seething waters of the Thames. The principal chamber, which we desire now to penetrate, was of unusually large dimensions, and was, by its monkish frequenters, learnedly designated the *Xenodochium*. This extensive hall was lofty, though somewhat sombre, being wholly floored and panelled with dark oak, save at the upper or raised end, where the walls were hung with grim-deviced tapestry, and the floor strewed with rushes.

On the day succeeding the important events discussed in our last chapters, and at the hour of one in the afternoon, there was congregated within this spacious chamber—as was the daily custom—an extraordinary assemblage of both sexes, engaged in feasting, revelling, singing, dicing, laughing, swearing, and other congenial amusements. Among the occupants were foreign merchants and traders, discussing their affairs somewhat rationally over stoups of Bordeaux, or other the wines of France and Spain, and with whom was a morisco, or wandering minstrel of Spain, with his viol-de-gamba; but the greater number of the roysterers and wassailers were composed of denizens of the precincts—friends and clients of the Black Friars.

These guests, among whom might be discerned several cowled figures, were waited upon by a number of tapsters, trencher scrapers, and drawers, under the lynx-eyed surveillance of the host, or inn-keeping Jove, who sat within an alcove at the far end in fat content and satisfaction.

All the manifold appliances of festivity were at hand. Pipes and rummers strewed the different boards. Perfume, subtle yet mellow, as of pine and lime, exhaled from out the numerous bowls, while savoury puffs flew up from the heated and well-cooked dishes, and, mingling with the subdued odours of the Indian weed, combined as delectable an atmosphere as any wassailer of those 'good old days' could have desired.

The " Three Bells " had, for a considerable period previously, in fact during the whole of the present Boniface's tenure, retained a high reputation for excellence as a restaurant and place of entertainment.　Taking all needful precaution to procure wines of the best vintages, he ever judiciously selected those most in vogue, among both the high and low degree of that age, and with his cellar so supplied, combined with a large stock of home-brewed nutty ales, ever in sound condition, he defied competition, and felt that the fortunes of his house and self were fairly made.

Having referred thus generally to the inn, its popularity, and its guests, we must more particularly regard those among the latter who play an essential part in our chronicle.　Sitting apart from the rest of the company, and within an alcoved window looking forth upon the green, and the glistening river beyond, and therein hidden purposely from those of the

guests who occupied the upper or more honourable end of the festal chamber, were two per-
sonages, who might well attract a lingering
notice, if not more marked attention, albeit they
were disguised, one in the dress of a Muscovite
merchant, with a long gown of brown cloth,
trimmed with red braid, a cap of black wolf's
skin, and a short crooked sword; the other in a
travelling cassock, completely enshrouding the
figure, and a calotte cap drawn so far over the
face as to make recognition almost impossible.
We have no disguise with our readers, and will
therefore listen awhile to their converse, carried
on, though it be, in a low tone.

"Albeit the drinks invented by man, while
nourishing the body, rack the soul, yet 'twere
prudent, gentle knight, if it be only to save
appearances, to order something of mine host,
who eyeth our abstinence somewhat sourly,"
said the Muscovite, who was no other than the
Maid of Kent.

"Thou sayest well, good Barton, and I'll
swagger it a bit. Ho, there! Harkee, tapster.

Bring hither some wine and freshment. I'd crush a flask of thy best Bordeaux with my comrade here," cried Richard Plantagenet.

" But listen, sir knight, for an I was now but telling you, none know, save myself, perhaps, that crabb'd monk's monstrous turpitudes," said Elizabeth Barton, with a gloomy visage, after the wine and accompaniments asked for had been served them.

" And are there then some direful secrets between thee Holy Maid, and that leprous Churchman ?" asked the knight in surprise.

" Lend me a patient ear, and I will expound this mystery, if one it really be," said Barton, in a dreamy dismal tone. " I will not be tedious to prate to you all the dark meetings and bleak discourses he and I once held, than which none direfuller in result to her most wrongfully designated ' holy ' were ever ordered among the despairing ones, in their hell-halls of eternal punishment."

She then drew the young knight closer to her, and, while shrouding her flame-burning face from all inspection, poured into his ear her

close-kept, dreary tale.   Having, in due course,
made an end, she wept such bitter tears that
they seemed to scorch the softness of her skin
as they fell.   This mood passed almost as
quickly as it came ; and then with earnestness,
and while her wondrous eyes flashed like meteors
of madness, she continued, " Thou thinkest,
sir knight, that I rave ; if you do, deem so yet
awhile."

" But can'st thou so drearily hate, where
once thou so fathomlessly loved ?" questioned
Plantagenet, in doubtful amaze.

" Hath the great archangel, since the day he
was banished forth of heaven, to prey on mankind, been received back again into the celestial
fold, or deem you he ever will ?   Methinks
'twere more in reason he should be again received into glory, than that traitorous monk
into my soul anew," cried Elizabeth Barton
with torrent-like vehemence.

" Can real love in woman so wholly fade as
to leave not a trace behind ?" added the knight
doubtingly.

" Hath not much, the labour of human hands

and human toil, perished for ever in the ages gone, leaving not a vestige to record its onetime fruitful existence? Can I, think you, obliterate the thought which glows like a ball of fire in my brain, and give its place once more, or ever again, to the soothing fantasies of love? Oh no! it hath become a hate which rankles ever in my soul, as some scarifying, unhealable wound; naught can stay it, naught vanquish it. No more could *he* bias me with all the wild terrors of his eloquence, who once held my very life in chains. He could win me, as well he knoweth, to no quality of forgiveness; for my spirit is exhausted of all but the hope and purpose of the vengeance I seek, in destroying his Church, and cleansing this land of those betraying abominations, yclept the monksties."

"But what said you, good Barton, of danger to my gentle Aveline? Methinks even villainy and outrage might respect such lily purity."

"Humanity will ever prey on itself, sir knight, like monsters of the deep, or beasts of the field. But hark to thy ear, thou hast a rival whose dark vigilance will never be long foiled."

" Ha! say you so, and in whom may I trace the black traitor ?" eagerly asked Plantagenet.

"In one even from whom I have felt the serpent's sting."

"What festering horror would you stir, Mistress Barton?   Speak not on such a matter o'er lightly, I beseech you."

" I only speak that which I know, dear youth," said Elizabeth Barton, eyeing her companion with an interest whose warmth there was no mistaking.   "More tales might be related of this monk's pleasurable disports than would furnish forth another set of amorous legends from a new Boccaccio — though, perchance, some would prove of too dark a dye to be ranked amid such sun-steeped reveries."

" He had best mind how he moves in this instance. If I do find him breathing aught un-churchmanly in his sweet pupil's ears, I'll unfrock and scourge him with his crime pub-lished on his back, through the streets of this

Nineveh.   But art thou in earnest, Barton, anent these serpent-like hints ?"

" Wherefore should I cozen you with idle words ? I have naught precise upon which I can bid you beware, but of a troth I would have thee impressed with the need for watch and caution. You love this desert flower, you behold her beauty, albeit you may not image fully the richness of the treasury which lays hidden in her heart and mind.   Guard her then as thou would'st thine own life.   But there is a still nigher danger, and for which to tell thee of I bid you hither."

" By St. George ! where lurketh then this new danger ?" asked the young knight, with a flash in his eye and a gush of fury through his heart.

" Yonder," answered the Maid of Kent, pointing significantly towards the upper end of the room.

" Ha ! say you so.   Methinks I recall his features.   Ay, 'tis he who would have outraged my sweet Aveline the other eve, and who, by my troth, yesterday so readily handled my gage. Will he, think you, pursue his evil intent further; or did he, as I supposed, but boast when he threatened ?"

" He, like his cruel sire, hath never been known to spare man or woman in his lust or passion," said the Maid slowly and somewhat sternly.

" 'Sdeath, I will to him at once, and do upon him the justice I was frustrated in the other eve, despite the haught station the chance boon of life hath assigned him. I will, by the mass, have his blood, ere he shall cast a blight upon the sweet flower Heaven hath given me !" exclaimed Plantagenet with flashing eyes, and hastily rising.

" Peace, knight. For the sake of her you love, be still. What canst thou hope to do against such odds as would meet you yonder at the first onslaught ? Be patient, and above all keep thy own counsel, and, perchance, you may be able to circumvent their dark purposes. But we have no time for these long pratings, for every instant that flies past heralds destiny. By your leave, sir knight, we will draw nigher, and if it be possible penetrate somewhat of their muttered discourse. Let us this way in the shadow, and withal with slow, thoughtful steps, else we may draw attention when most we want it afar. Our Lady be praised, they heed us not! Here are seats, close beneath their table."

Round the board at this the upper end of the spacious hall—always retained for those lordly and honoured guests, or ruffling gallants, who from time to time frequented the famed hospice of the "Three Bells"—were seated a party of five. The board literally groaned beneath the numerous assortment of provisions provided to stay the pangs of their appetites. There were chines of beef, roasted pig, cold brawn, huge pasties of pigeon and venison, trenchers of stewed hare, roasted duck, buttered crab, manchets of flour, salads of salmon, and other dainties. Long-necked flasks placed in coolers, with a numerous array of flagons, tankards, and glasses filled up the vacant spots on the snow-white cloth.

The cheer thus provided was evidently appreciated by the party assembled to do it honour, for an evidencing silence of the tongue had, for a considerable time, reigned amid the clatter of plates and knives, and the rattling and jingling of flagons and glasses. This hungry calm was at last broken by him who seemed to be the giver of the feast, and the most haught and noble among the party—a tall, stout, florid, handsome cavalier, dressed in the extreme fashion of court costume.

" Gadzooks, Master Boniface is a *rara avis*, albeit he is honest as times go; for, beshrew me, he knoweth well how to provide for stomach cravings. I know not the time when we feasted more to our hearts' content. Ho! ho there! Ralph Stephen, worthy host, a bottle of thy choicest Burgundy to wash clear the flavour of yon savoury pasty with its salletting."

The bottle was forthwith produced, followed by another, and yet another. Wines were superfluities in those days, and their prices would astonish the wealthy connoisseurs of this high-priced age. Imagine an enactment being passed, limiting the price of all French wines to *eightpence a gallon*, and Malmsey and Romsey sacks, and other sweet wines, to *one shilling*.

"Thunder and bombards! the grape that yielded so luscious a juice, ought to be for ever immortalized; for Bacchus never brewed better," said he whose words we have previously noted, after a deep draught of the purple liquor. "They who make the 'Three Bells' of Blackfriars their headquarters, choose a spot scarce short of paradise. How say you, Sadler; bethink you Wolsey might have chanced upon a worse hostelry in his enforced banishment?"

"His Grace's reign is ended, and we might do worse, your Highness, than drink his health beneath the frown which fortune hath capped his pride withal," answered Sir Ralph Sadler.

"By my father's beard that will we! But hark to thy ear, friend of mine, I am in hopes my royal sire, albeit so chary of his cash, will allot me the lieutenancy of Calais now vacant by Wolsey's fall, sithence I am so vexed and stung by those damnable gadflies — a man's creditors. But to thy toast. Ho there, drawers! Ho! I say, ye lazy varlets, fill high, and to the brim o'erflowing; for we will all drink lustily to the health of him who, albeit his pride and his power, hath most surely mightily fallen. There shall be a merry world in England again since the unmatched schoolmaster hath at last quitted his lofty stool. So drink, my comrades, drink deep to the health of the mighty fallen— Wolsey by name."

And drunk was the health with all the manifold honours pertaining to a clamorous, hard-drinking set.

"How think you, royal Perrot, will the Cardinal's abasement, and our royal master's zealous inroads upon the convents, open up to our aspiring energies any sensuous food? Methinks there are buxom harems enow to be selected from nunneries," said a young and handsome man, elaborately decked in courtly garniture, and who was no other than Herbert, Earl Pembroke, who thereafter rose to great wealth, power, and influence.

"Ho, by my fay, 'tis likely enow!   Thou

canst have thy choice when thou listest in that case, Pembroke.   Mine is made; and naught so sweet ever yet lived and bloomed beneath the azure of the heavens," said Sir John Perrot, with a flaming visage.

"I felt something akin to sorrow, when Wolsey bowed his head so humbly. 'Twas a healless wound dealt him, which will lurk at his soul till death relieves him," said Sadler, with a half sigh.

"Now, out on thee, Ralph! Art turned misanthrope? Cog'sbones! Wolsey was one, I do avouch, who knew well how to combine in a high degree the *suaviter in modo* with the *fortiter in re*.   But for all that, there was no stamen in his wisdom, which was, of a verity, all head and no body, like the pictures of the Goddess Laverna; or, mayhap, at the best, all head and shoulders like a codfish.   But I forget what 'tis far more important I should remember, this eve must behold me master of my sweet mistress, and that too, with thy good help Sadler."

"Art not loath to meddle further in that

matter, Perrot, sithence you may draw that young fire-eating monk-knight upon thee again ?" said Sadler, with a half smile.

" How mean you ? Shall I be thwarted and turned from my purpose by a boy like that, half monk and whole malapert though he be. By my fay ! I will teach him what 'tis to meddle, and will, by my troth ! make him cry mercy when we joust together at Whitehall," exclaimed Sir John Perrot.

" I mislike not his appearance or his spirit," persisted Sadler, with the same smile. " He beareth himself nobly. Look at his raven locks, his front like Jove's, his ' eye like Mars to threaten and command,' and all his full-length graces matchless as Hyperion's."

" Go to, Sadler, go to, I say. Thou wilt not match the beardless, unformed youth against my ripeness, I trow," retorted Sir John Perrot, with a haught laugh. " Hark thee, to thy ear, we must perchance, or perforce, carry off this damsel ere another sunrise streaks the earth."

" I am with your Highness, to do and dare

as an thou needest. But art fully prepared on
all points ? For well I trow, the fair damsel will
not go with thee as a lamb to the slaughter."

" God's life ! yonder are my staunch swash-
bucklers, the trusty Captain Roche, *le filou sans
peur et sans reproche*, and his no less active lieutenant, Tony Vulp ; and with their aid need I of
a surety no further preparation," said Sir John,
looking towards the end of the board, where
sat the two worthies he referred to, involved in
a deep-muttered conversation, while imbibing
pretty freely of the spirituous nectars set before
them. The one designated Captain Roche
was a handsome man, with a striking physi-
ognomy, albeit wonderfully dark and sinister in
expression. His eyes were black, remarkably
penetrating, and glowed with the fiercest fire
when kindled by passion. His hair was coal
black, and hung in long wavy masses over his
neck and shoulders. His dress was rich, though
sober in colouring, being altogether of dark
assortment. We will not weary the reader's
patience with long personal descriptions, but

will sum up by stating that this notable personage was a fit companion for all deeds of
fierce daring or ruthless adventure. His
heart ever appeared of adamant, utterly impenetrable to any gentle emotion, while his arm
was of iron, ready and able to second all his
soul prompted. His companion, or lieutenant,
one Tony Vulp, was a far more disagreeable
looking personage. With sunken cunning grey
eyes, which were either bloodshot by dissipa-
tion, or reddened by the fire of innate cruelty,
au aquiline nose that gave a hawklike expression to his face, thick, coarse, sensuous lips, a
long wiry moustache and beard, which, like
his shaggy mane, were of a fiery red, the casual
observer must needs have shuddered at the
villainous aspect, the low combination of face
and feature, thus presented to view. Indeed a
countenance more expressive of, or a heart more
replete with cunning and knavery than that of
Tony Vulp's it would be difficult to discover.
He was much shorter than the other—who was
tall, well and powerfully made—but, for all that,

his large muscular development demonstrated he was no unworthy helpmate for his employer, Captain Roche.   Both were heavily armed.

" Look that thou keep this secret, Vulp, or I will force a padlock on your tongue you shall not of a surety unlock!" exclaimed Captain Roche, in a murmur that sounded like distant thunder.

" Hist!   But I tell you Captain, we must be up and stirring, if you wish to lay thy clutch on the gold," retorted the other in subdued tones.

" Where say you he keepeth it?" asked Roche.

" In the well, within the very centre of the castle—a rare place for exorcising spirits.   We must seek his treasures just ere sunrise, or perchance we may be torn to bloody atoms by fiends who it is avouched act as his familiars."

" Get thee gone for a fool, to list to such old women's tales," retorted Captain Roche disdainfully.

" Think as you will, captain, I will not, by the cross of God! venture within his clutch or theirs, save at the hours they dare not exercise their mislawful calling!" said Vulp determinedly, who, though he usually drank like a fish, and swaggered and swore like twenty troopers, was a very coward in cold blood, and was, moreover, a marvellous believer in the general superstitions of the age—which may be justly denominated one in which " prodigies and signs abortive, presages and tongues of Heaven," had each and all their interpreters—an age when omens furnished our greatest historians and poets with subjects of the noblest imagery—an age, too, when all that was imaginary and superstitious was held to firmly.

" Thou art ill and aguish, or getting old and unfit for daring deeds, to be thus unwholesomely scared," said Captain Roche, with a very undisguised sneer, while mixing in a large goblet two kinds of wine—Burgundy and Alicant —and then draining them at a draught.

" Though I would face not him who is akin to the devil, I natheless lack not fire and courage to wield a sword when you bid it forth of the scabbard. But mayhap you never heard, captain, that it is veraciously reported, that when Master Verstegans, as a child, was held by his godmother at the font, the holy water hissed when it fell upon his little face, as upon glowing coals."

"By Lot's youngest daughter! the fairest wench ever created, what a tale to affright children in daylight!" commented Captain Roche impatiently. "Harkee Vulp, he may be the strangest rat ever cast forth of creation, I care not; but, so soon as we have done the service we are wanted for by our noble employer yonder, I will test Raimond Verstegans' powers whilome we filch his gold."

"Thou wilt not do it without his cognizance, if all be true Dame Rumour doth wantonly whisper abroad," said Vulp, leaning over to his companion, and lowering still further his voice. "By St. Botolph! it is presumed this Magian hath a rare crystal, which he weareth constantly about his person, and which, on observation, warns him, by its dimness or brightness, whether danger is at hand or afar; and moreover he hath a dog, foaled of a lion's whelp, which hath the discernment and strength of a dozen men, and which is his weird familiar."

" Out on thee, purblind dolt, for such craven fancies! Warned or not warned, dog or no dog, I am bent on supplying my necessities from the superabundant store in, as ye say, the castle well. These black phantoms concerning Raimond Verstegans scare thee belike ; but they inkle naught in my heart, who am ever ready to dare the more when evil or danger the worse grows," said Captain Roche, with a fierce growl.

" Let be! Though you doubt that whereof I tell you, I will natheless be thy accompaniment to the weirdman's abode; and, while ransacking his treasures, thou mayest see and believe with your own eyes. Meanwhile let be, and tip me a jorum," persisted Tony Vulp somewhat sullenly, while leaning back on his ample seat.

" Dost know the way to this unlikely spot— this enchanted well of thine."

" I know not the direct one ; but that by

which I will lead you, my noble captain, though certes dark, long, and belike ill-favoured, is the safest, and altogether free from espial, unless, perchance, witchcraft expose us."

"Peace, thou superstitious tramontane, peace! See you not Sir John beckons for our approach?" exclaimed Captain Roche, swallowing a final bumper, and then rising, he strode to the upper end of the board.

"Art well attuned for active service, well muscled for sword-wielding, Roche?" demanded Sir John Perrot in a significant tone.

"You'll find no fitter man in the whole of broad England, for all services requiring courage, daring, and strength, than I," returned the captain, drawing up his broad, towering figure, and looking the perfection of manly form and power.

"Thou art no braggart, an I believe you, Roche, and art made of the stuff I need in my designs. Art sure, though, of thy fellow?" questioned Sir John, eyeing Vulp with no very flattering thoughts.

"Content you, my lord; he is but my second sword. He doeth what he perceives I require of him," answered Captain Roche, with a fierce grin.

" Why, God-a-mercy, a useful knave, and a burly one to boot !" cried the disguised nobleman. " He would amaze my royal sire, with his knotty sinews and iron-turned muscles. He is not, I trust, o'er riotous in his cups. But, hark ye, Captain Roche, our venture must be perfected this eve."

" I am ever ready, as accordeth with my motto," said Roche, whose air and manner, though soldierly and stately, were reckless and *blasé*, and at times even roughly abrupt, although not altogether displeasant.

" By the faith of my body, my motto hath a more prudent smatter about it; for doth it not read after monkish fashion, ' *Turris prudentia custos !* ' " cried the Earl of Pembroke. " But, Perrot, thou wilt assuredly be led to thy ruin by Evekind. Dost forget it has been well written :—

" He ploughs in the waves, and sows in the sand,
And strives to catch the vagabond winds in nets,
Who founds his hopes in woman's heart or hand."

"Thou art an infidel, Herbert, to prate thus of woman. I should feel disposed to do thee battle on their behalf, did I not know your heart gainsays what your tongue hath so idly uttered," exclaimed Sir Ralph Sadler jeeringly.

Meanwhile Sir John Perrot had conveyed his instructions to Captain Roche and his lieutenant, the latter of whom, after some muttered conversation, exclaimed with a fierce growl, "If he interferes, by God's wounds! I'll slit his ears, cut his throat, and throw his carcase to some dog to lick clean for his shroud; though I be thereafter compelled to eat the friars' scraps in this sanctuary the rest of my days!"

"Peace, bull-dog! Faith and troth thou art enow to ruin the devices of Solomon!" exclaimed Sir John.

"Leave the sequel to me, your Grace," said Captain Roche, in a low impressive whisper. "This young knight shall be punished to your heart's content."

"Nay, nay; harm him not save with the neces-

sary handling to keep him beyont interference.
I'll myself settle accounts with him and, gadzooks! after my own fashion," said Sir John
Perrot, after an instant's struggle of warring
feeling. "So, harm him not, I say, lest ye seek
to incur my displeasure. But how say you,
Captain Roche, where and when shall we unite
our forces ?"

"Leave the proceedings within these exempt
precincts to me. Body-o'-me, I'll care for all
that is here needful to be done ! I will under-
take to secure the lady; and as, mayhap, it would
not be safe to escort her through either of the
land entrances, we will e'en depart with her by
water, from the pier in front of this hostelry.
Your Grace had best be in waiting for us, with
led horses and such like, beside the stairs in
the Alsatia of Whitefriars, at what hour you
may-like name."

"So be it, and let the hour of rendezvous be
eight of the clock this eve. I trust all, then, to
your aidance, Roche; and hark ye, perform what
you have undertaken, and a hundred nobles

shall be your remuneration—a no bad reward as times go."

"Content you! It shall all be done as your Grace listeth."

"Grace!—me no grace on such random adventures as these. *Ventre bleu!* mind thou that, Roche. I am simple Sir John Perrot at yours or anybody's service—at least, so long as it pleaseth us," exclaimed the disguised scion of royalty with haughty vehemence. "But whom have we here, listening so perkily, with all his ears in the stubble?" he added, turning and catching sight of Richard Plantagenet, who, in spite of all the Maid's entreaties, had risen, and was gazing with flaming eyes and hostile mien at the wild and reckless speaker.

"One who hath proved your master ere now, and who thou must needs o'ercome ere thou canst in a tittle achieve thy dark purposes. So look to it, thou roysterer, whom men call Perrot. By St. George! I know you now, and sooner, I trow, than either of us well weeted," cried the young knight with angry vehemence.

" 'Sblood! prithee have patience, sir springald.

We'll meet at the tournay; and, by the mass, when we do, look to it, for, ere we part again, I trust to handle thee in a way to serve thy turn for a season, as cutting thy throat would for all eternity!" answered Sir John Perrot, with a disdainful smile.

"It shall be seen how far thine arm canst make good thy boasts. I will leave thee no strength to serve thee another turn, so help me God, at the day of doom!" retorted Plantagenet vehemently, allowing himself to be drawn away by his more cautious companion.

"What evil hap hath brought that young cat-a-mountain among us!" exclaimed Sir John Perrot testily.

"Be avised, Perrot, give up this pursuit; it will but lead to worse mischief. Women are not so scarce, I trow, that man need confine himself to one object; and mind you the doggrel, not for amiss in cases such as thine :

> "For in the rose there was a wasp
> Which stung his nose, to smell—to smell,
> And then he blamed the rose—the rose
> And flung it in—a well."

·' Out on thee, Ralph, for a persistent
vilifier. Gad's life! you should enlist among
the friar preachers; for thou art out of tune
for such company as this. I'm resolved, *coûte
qui coûte*, the girl shall be mine, despite her
womanish fantasies, or you youth's unmannerly
deportment. Who shall gainsay me — ha!"
with some asperity exclaimed Sir John Perrot,
who, need we add, did not belie his royal parent-
age in loving the jovial chase, the nightly revel,
and the blooming maid. Of a truth he adored
Beauty and verily made a deity of Love.

CHAPTER II.

The Wave of the Cataract.

"IT is my evil hap ever to encounter obstacles, where most my heart craves supremity!" exclaimed the young knight passionately, as with his companion, the Maid of Kent, he left the 'Three Bells,' and threaded the narrow and intricate thoroughfares of the Wilderness towards the Manor-house.

"Thou hast those to oppose you whose fellness has, I trow, been long a ripening. Of a surety shouldst thou know ere this not to trust to fair seeming, much less to mortal man. He who holds to man's faith but places his footsteps on the sands of time. But as we must not, I deem, apply the higher powers of the microscope to human handicraft, if we would not behold it coarse and uneven, so certes must we refrain from dwelling o'er critically on human excellences. We might in good troth magnify a flower, or a feather, or a shell, or any other creation of Nature's God, but we must needs admire the work of human toil and ingenuity with the naked eye. So of a surety does it not answer, I well weet, to hold up man's worth to too strong a light, nor weight his charity in too nice a balance."

" How mean you, Mistress Barton ?" questioned Plantagenet with some curiosity.

" I hold no special thesis. I mean but this, dear youth, that in the evil thy foes would work thee, they act but on passions common, mayhap, to all mankind," returned Elizabeth Barton mildly.

" What! call you it right or honourable, or worthy a truculent churchman to hold the designs you assert Dan Theodulph hath in his mind, against the angel peace and purity of Mistress More ; or that a knight and noble of high degree should persecute her foully, so o'er much 'gainst her will ? Call ye such intents and doings common to our race? Wouldst thou deraign them? Out on thee, lady, for so foul a charge against all manhood and honour!" exclaimed the knight impetuously.

"I deem you right, more certainly so as regards the voluptuous pursuits of that honey-tongued traitor Dan Theodulph. Lovers' eyes, they assert, are of far vision; see that yours are ever so. Let it pass. We cannot help, natheless, the operations of feeble judgment or morbid vanity, nor of a surety can we hinder such mental diseases, betraying themselves in violent language, fierce hatreds, and perchance more vigorous animosities. For mind you, sir knight, nothing is too fierce for a fanatic, or too false for a hypocrite, as may be daily witnessed," said the Maid of Kent, in a dizzy and shaken voice.

"Why keep you secret the dark plottings and diablerie of this leprous monk? Render him to judgment and punishment. I espy no good reason why thou shouldst longer conceal his amazing turpitude," said the knight impatiently.

" Nay, sir knight. It is not of a troth mine province to destroy. I would, with Heaven's will, the rather save," replied the Maid in a tremulous tone. " But heed not those passages of my past existence you wot well I related solely to thy confidence. Our whole life is a troubled volume, of which each successive leaf seems more bleakly filled. But I am, albeit certain dark thoughts which make me shiver, despite the sun, still nerved to encounter, as resignedly as may be, all the ills a most untoward destiny may yet have in store for me, and oft in fancy do I behold spectral illusions of coming trials, which well-nigh turn my heart to stone. Oh ! that I was even now numbered amid those blest martyrs who have already sunk to eternal rest, ere their country's sun shall set in clouds blood-red with the oppression and treachery now dawning."

" Why, in God's troth, indulge in such dreary fantasies ? Why not, Mistress Barton, breathe more of hope, until worse proof hap to the contrary ?"

" Hast ever marked these lines, sir knight ?

" I have thought
Too long and darkly, till my brain became,
In its own eddy boiling and o'erwrought,
A whirling gulf of phantasy and flame."

But I forget, it is not well akin to my duty to wrangle thus mournfully of myself. My business on earth now is to root out so far as I may the black plants that choke this fair land with evil superstitions," continued the Maid somewhat bewilderedly.

" Prithee beware, Mistress Barton, of the thorny path you have chosen. I am not all untaught, as perchance you deem, in the doctrines you cling to, and so openly breathe abroad. Oh ! take heed unto thyself; for well I wot that for saying but little more than thou declarest did Raphael Roodspere suffer at the blazing stake. I would not behold thy goodly form scathed in the cruel flames," said the young knight gently.

" Fear not for me, dear knight. Let the poor enginery I can command plead with thee, to fully believe in that blessed teaching which hath already glimmered in your soul, and so permit me to lead you more securely on that path of light which hath of late been pioneered to the skies."

" Be it so, good Barton ; albeit not now. At a fitter season I will hear thee. I must now needs hasten to take such precautions as may be needful for the earthly weal of Mistress More," said Richard Plantagenet, as they arrived within sight of the old mansion, whither he was bound.

" Be secret, be wary! But deem not I prate at all seasons tidings of wanhope and despair. A new creation is dawning, live thou to inherit it and be blest, remembering the while that the mercy of God is greater than the evil-doing of man, in proportion as the boundless skies are broader than the spanned earth," exclaimed Elizabeth Barton, as she took her leave, and with a look which that complex and wonderful mirror of the human soul hath rarely expressed, so full were her splendid orbs of an infinitude of contending emotions.

While she strode slowly and thoughtfully away towards the thickly populated districts of the wilderness, there to preach the solemn truths, and still more solemn warnings of the glorious mission with which she had yoked herself withal, the young knight speeded on his way, and erelong stood within the presence of her who had become the light and life of his being. His heart glowed as if with living fire when he beheld her, and when he perceived that upon her face a mystic smile played like a butterfly over the deepening roses of her cheeks on the moment when her love-thralled soul felt his approach. She rose quickly though gracefully to meet him, all her motions undulating as if to some internal music of enjoyment and happiness.

She wore a plain morning costume, and her countenance, when again it settled to its former hue, was pale as the snowdrop in the bright moonlight, albeit as beautiful and attractive as ever. Her attitude, too, became once more drooping and powerless; while a deep shade of despondency, as of some unseen presence of evil, clouded her beauty like twilight from the valley of death, penetrating beyond its own ordained limits, far into the sunnier atmosphere of earth. He questioned her as to the cause with a lover's anxiety and eagerness. She answered him with gentle fervour, and with a tenderness like the all-melting warmth of sunset's golden air. But why should we attempt to pry into those deep, fervent thoughts, which for the nonce flooded their souls like purple seas.

Imbued with much of the antique spirit of chivalry, which, to a great extent, influenced the age in which he lived, young Richard Plantagenet was ready and able to pay fervent homage to his sweet mistress's sovereign beauty, and to maintain its supremacy against all questioners, while he was wholly incapable of worshipping at any meaner shrine. And now, when he felt that danger menaced her, and violence was abroad to do her wrong; his spirit was up in arms, and, of a surety, eager for the fray, so long as his sword might be drawn in defence of her person or her honour.

"Thou lovest me, sweet Aveline. I worship thee," he cried in a rapturous ecstacy. "But, sweet one, I should feel better assured, and could encounter fate more cheerfully, an I knew that thou wert safe from every harm."

They loved each other, gentle, noble, un-matched pair. Their love, too, was not the tainted, effete passion, that sways men and women in these material and worldly-minded times. It was a feeling suitable to those more primitive days—days of generous impulses and noble deeds—not found on this harsh and every-day earth. It was love's poesy, belonging of right to the Saturnian age, and to the dreams of demigod and nymph.

They were enthralled with the elysium of their mutual thoughts and feelings—with the matchless happiness which, in their fore-shadowed union, appeared to court their accept-ance. The sweetness of the flowery essences which surrounded them, and the bright effulgence of the sunlit hour, well suited their amorous converse ; and time passed with the vivid rapidity of all things delightful in this world of mortal life and mortal suffering. For the nonce dwelling in a new Eden of their own creation, they deemed not they were in the world, until recalled from the heaven they worshipped to the earth they feared. An intruder, in the person of Master Secretary Cromwell, broke upon their sunlit wilderness of flowering hopes.

" Ha ! Master Cromwell, whom seek you, and of what colour are your news," exclaimed the young knight, with some slight show of impatience at the interruption.

" I have somewhat of import to disclose to my lord prior at the monastery, and need thy accompaniment," returned Cromwell, with a glance of warm interest at the young pair.

" How so, Master Secretary ? What have I to do with thee or thy disclosures ?" demanded Plantagenet impatiently.

" Much that will in due course be known. Wilt come and learn, or bide here, and let love ruin thee and thy mistress beyond all redeeming," said Cromwell, with some earnestness.

" Out on thee for a troublesome intruder! I will with thee, natheless. So set on, I will join you ere you have trodden many paces," said Plantagenet; and, as Master Cromwell departed, he again turned towards Aveline, who was gazing on him with an expression of devoted tenderness that stirred his soul to its lowest depths, so sweet and penetrating was its subtle flame.

He again impressed upon her the warning he had previously enjoined, to keep, for the most part, within doors, or when she went abroad, even though it were only to take exercise in the garden, to be accompanied by one or more of the servitors well armed for any unruly or hostile emergency. He then commended her to the care of all blessed spirits, and promising to return ere night had fully fallen, he departed in pursuit of Master Cromwell, whom he found awaiting him without any signs of impatience, at the wicket leading into the

Wilderness. This they, in due course, threaded, Cromwell abstaining from satisfying the curiosity of his young companion, until they reached the monastery, and were forthwith inducted to the presence of Prior Struddell, whom they found engaged with Dan Theodulph, and a tall, dark, ominous-looking ecclesiastic, no other than Tunstall, Bishop of Durham, formerly of London, and then keeper of the Privy Seal.

The sub-prior at once departed, bowing with froward meekness to Cromwell, but fixing on Plantagenet a glance of his keen eyes, full of a vague, unfathomable, and almost terrible expression, which haunted the young knight for long after.

"I bid thee farewell, my lord prior. Thou wilt do well to assure thyself of thy subordinate's discharge of our instructions concerning this damsel, whom people of our time fanatically designate, 'Holy Maid of Kent,' while I will order strict search to be instituted for such copies of Tyndale's translations as your informant announces to be within this new and sinful

Nineveh," said Tunstall in his deep, impressive tones.

"Do so, my lord, and I will take heed, when thou hast them accounted for, to make public reproof, by their destruction without our precincts, as I purpose with some already safely housed, the day beyont to-morrow. These heretical publications shall be consumed by fire, as thou mayest witness an thou wilt, by way of stern warning to those tainted with the errors of that Satanic root of the heresy of the Bohemians, surnamed Wicliffe," said the lord prior with considerable asperity.

"I know not how that may be," returned Tunstall. "But let be; sufficient for the day is the evil thereof. I must now away, time flies, and with his enigmatical scythe warns me not to waste the hours that remain, not knowing of a surety when we may be called upon to account for their misuse. Jesu therefore be with you, and our Blessed Lady support you. Ha! Master Cromwell, I greet you. *Benedicite!*" And this distinguished prelate also departed.

Prior Struddell, after the usual formal salutations had been gone through, gazed with ill-concealed anxiety on Cromwell's face, as he demanded, in his usual mild impressive manner, " And what brings his Grace's Secretary of Laws so soon again to our poor house of the Friar preachers ?"

" Call me no longer by that designation, an it please you, my lord prior. Human greatness is naught but a phantom—a temple gorgeous, mayhap, though raised on shifting sands. There is no more a secretary of laws to his Grace, for his Eminence is no longer such," said Cromwell with manifest perturbation.

" What! Hath the great Cardinal—the Pope's vicegerent, indeed fallen?" exclaimed Prior Struddell aghastly ; for though Wolsey's persistent tournay against the power, influence, and very existence of the religious houses had done much to lessen his majesty and authority among them, yet could they not view his fall, as the representative, in this country, of the great Head of their Church, save as another sign and token of those portentous changes which, they too plainly discerned, threatened them, and which in their growth and subsequent ascension would infallibly overwhelm them all in a destructive, uncontrollable flood of ruin. We may here state that part of Wolsey's intended policy was—the King remarried to some one of his selection, and the succession settled—to purge the Church of England of much of its grossness and superstition, and to convert the largest monasteries throughout the kingdom into intellectual garrisons of pious and learned men. But this, with the whole fabric of Pride, Power, and Ambition, had come to a sudden end, and the barriers which Wolsey's single hand had upheld immediately gave way, the flood had free scope, and he himself was the first to be swept away amid the *débris.* And when, in the course of a few days, the intelligence was disseminated that he had sunk into his last sleep, where the grievous burthen of office and the load of obloquy could oppress him no more, none wondered, and few pined, while, as a striking commentary, the King was immediately declared by the voice of Parliament to be " Protector and only Supreme Head of the Church and clergy of England."*

" The King hath with his own hand stricken to the dust the goodly power he had one time raised to almost celestial majesty. Wolsey, my lord and master, whom ever I served and honoured, is no more, save in name; and that e'en I trow will not be for long, so ill-prepared is his haught spirit to bear up against such an overwhelming reverse," added Cromwell, with considerable emotion.

" Methought it would so come to pass, when I beheld how his Eminence withstood the wrong anent the divorce, so determined on by the King in the court but yesterday," added the prior, in a low, mournful tone.

" Ay, ay! 'twas his mishap to beard his master so; for look you, my lord prior, our im-

* Burnet, vol. iii., p. 78.

perious sovereign is little apart from a madman when he is sorely vexed," said Cromwell.

" 'Tis wondrous strange his Eminence knew not better how to order his speech and decretal in so gainsaying his king. Well I ween, to enable humanity to use power, and yet restrain it from abusing it, hath ever proved a vain attempt to the dreamer, and certes to the practical man a far aloof ordainment, which, though always to be kept in vision's range, yet forsooth is never to be attained—a very lighthouse, but natheless no haven. It is ever—ever thus. The lighthouses of experience are erected in vain for humanity—tossed and driven on its tumultuous seas of passion. Alas! alas! and is the great Cardinal himself fallen and brought low ?" said Prior Struddell, in tremulous wonderment.

" Ay, even so, my lord prior. He is stricken by him he only too well served; even as his own heart in its bitterness exclaimed, 'Oh! had I but served my God as I have served my king, He would not have abandoned me in my old days so utterly. Only remorse and sorrow remain to me of all my glorious past!"

"Spake his Grace thus?" asked the prior, with a heavy sigh.

"Even so, my lord. He is fallen, and indeed altogether broken in spirit and form. But though he be so, of his deeds will I ever avouch the truth, as freely as streams percolate their waters through rocks," said Cromwell, with fervour.

"Oh! who that thus witnesseth the fall in ruins of so gorgeous a temple, can comprehend what secret undermining hath removed its one-time stout props? He will perish, not so his fame. His body will become but a mere rotten reed upon an eternal shore of silence; but his memory will shine as a brilliant far-off star, throughout future generations," exclaimed the prior, with enthusiasm.

"In very faith thou hast scanned the truth. E'en do I who, as his constant associate, hath had the best means of proof, know that his Grace did ever disdain that ephemeral notoriety with which privileged people are, I trow, apt to surround thrones, that he might of a troth await that popularity, which time will e'en develop, and which of a surety posterity will consecrate," added Cromwell, with genuine warmth.

"Though he hath wronged our ancient institution, yet ever hath he wrought the service of the Holy Catholic Church. So let him rest on the throne of his own high deeds—let him still greet existence, albeit he willingly awaits death. *In Christo mori est vivere,*"* said the prior calmly.

"Thou must not imagine thy Church or thy institutions will pass henceforth scatheless, because the mighty purger hath departed from the scene of his incessant labours. His task hath assuredly descended to other though less worthy hands; but your Augean stable will yet of a surety be cleansed and remodelled, if Thomas Cromwell hath aught of power in the

* Old monastic proverb.

new office this morn hath seen thrust upon him."

"What mean you — what further hath happed?" demanded the prior, with outward calmness, though with a pallid face and a strange foreboding at his heart.

"Nothing more, forsooth, than that the high offices so worthily held by his Grace the Cardinal are all separated, and less worthily placed, I am well minded. Cranmer is raised to the highest step in his ladder, for he hath e'en been installed Archbishop of Canterbury."

"That is no good boding for our Holy Church," interposed the prior.

"Worse hath yet to be said on that score, my lord. Sir Thomas More, a man in all wise fit, is chosen Lord Chancellor."

"*Deo gratias!* He will do justice for truth's and his conscience' sake. He is a worthy man and to be trusted," said Prior Struddell.

"Your humble servant, Thomas Cromwell, hath been knighted, and made one of the Privy

Council," continued the late secretary of laws with a grim smile.

" Thou art no friend of ours, Master Cromwell, I am not now to learn. Thou wouldst, no doubt, sooner behold this land a Golgotha, an Aceldama, a field of blood, hopelessly entangled in bitter contention and everlasting warfare, than for the sake of peace and goodwill among the families of earth support that Church which hath throughout ages proved itself the only true ordainment of God," said the prior, somewhat impatiently.

" If He who made all creation commands, who of mortal mould dare disobey? I am self-warned as to the course I must needs pursue; and prithee, my lord prior, when speaks the Almighty more clearly than in the living hearts of men ?" said Cromwell, slowly and sternly.

" Beware of the path whereon you would tread, Master Cromwell; 'tis full of fiery danger, not only to your soul's weal, but e'en to your bodily wholeness. Full many, I trow, have suffered as heretics ere now," exclaimed the prior, in a warning voice.

"Take heed to thyself—threaten not me. 'Tis more against your foul, leprous, monachal institutions I am up in arms than against your Church. It hath been well asserted, ' Shrink to the clergy and they be lions; lay their faults roundly and charitably to them and they be as sheep,'"* retorted Cromwell, warily.

"Thou canst not speed thy heretical illwill against our harbours of refuge, unless God for his own good purposes sanctions the desecration," exclaimed Prior Struddell, with some warmth.

"Hath it ta'en long, nay more than a few short months, think you, to bring down the great superstition of ages, you and all monkhood reverence, from the towering eminence whereon it once stood with every outward sign of unparalleled prosperity, and to suspend it beside the brink of a precipice of which no living man

* State Papers.

can fathom the depth. Mark me, my lord prior, and bear well my words in mind ; your institution is doomed, and not long shall it be before all vestiges of its one time fruitful existence shall be swept for ever away in the full flood of that stream which is now setting in to destroy the Goliah of Rome in this land—that foundation whereon ye of the cowl have raised your houses of sin and superstition," urged Cromwell, carried away in spite of his usual precautionary judgment.

"Well may it be urged that the fiend hath temptations adapted to all human moods," said the prior with a gloomy sigh. " But our Blessed Lady forbid that I should adjudge your heresy or your wrong-doing. God, the sovereign arbiter of the life of man, oft raises up one to punish the crimes of many, as we of the cloister may experience in our decline and ruin. *Benedicamus Domino nostro.* His will be done on earth as it is in heaven. Let our institution be blotted out from the state of being, who, prithee Master Cromwell, amongst the generations yet unborn, will not recur with just admiration to the long, time-honoured narratives of the heroic age of Monasticism? Thou wilt, too, so consider ere thy time hast fully sped, albeit you smile now. Forget not, in thy antagonism, that our primæval houses were from the first regarded as peaceful refuges for the oppressed; very havens in the wide, stormy social sea; lamps of learning to lighten the weight of ignorance which reigned around; happy penfolds where childhood in troublous times might chaunt its blitheness while studying art, science, or craft; peaceful refuges for old age, when it had battled through the myriad vicissitudes of life, and sought quiet to prepare itself for the world to come. Ever, too, hath our holy army filled up its ranks as well from those of servile condition as from freemen; while also have been readily admitted men from rustic life, laborious professions, and from plebeian labours. No enquiry was ever sought, whether the novice was rich or poor, bond or free, young or old; for neither age nor condition were ever matters of consideration, certes, among us of the cloister.   But surely have all our virtues, all our good works, sunk for naught in the great waters of oblivion; and well hath our doom been foreshadowed in the prophetic lays of the old poets, even of the Augustan day. But e'en though our hour be far or nigh, we must not complain, nor cease for a moment our labours in the great field of truth.   Men die.   Nations rise and fall.   But humanity careers ever onward in its mighty course.   Well we know that the battle is not always to the strong, but that as the moon wanes, only there-after to renew her glory, so is the tendency of all human events towards a triumphant con-clusion.   Do you, Master Cromwell, and you, my dear son, Plantagenet, as well also all future posterity, understand that the principles that lie, of a troth, at the root of our monastic sys-tem, fully enter into, and are, in fact, borrowed from the organization of human society, while they aptly illustrate the theory of the higher Christian dogmas.   But I have done.   Thou camest not hitherward to hear a lecture or bide reproof. Our days on earth are as a shadow, and there is none abiding. As human life is in the hands of the Redeemer, so also are all humanly constituted fabrics, and therefore, with him, and in his hands, is the future fate of Monachism." He paused for a moment, and, ere Cromwell could reply, he demanded of the latter the precise cause of his visit.

"Ha! that minds me well, my lord prior, that I have not avised thee of the greatest event which hath ta'en place since his Grace the Cardinal's fall—the Lady Anne, Marchioness of Pembroke, whom the king, on some won-drous goodly night* had, it seems, in secrecy married, hath been this morn publicly declared, both without the Palace of Bridewell and that of York House—to be hereafter termed White-hall—his queen; and for her coronation as such proclamation is now being made, ordering its taking place on the fifth day from hence."

* St. Paul's Day, 1533.

" O blessed Jesu ! can such ill tidings have truly oozed forth to the light?" questioned Prior Struddell in doubtful amaze.

" Thou mayest, perchance, have time e'en now to hear the heralds making proclamation without the palace of Bridewell, an thou wouldst journey to the tower beside your great fore-gate," answered Cromwell.

" Nay, it needs not. I am assured of thy veracity, albeit not of thy faith or goodwill," said Prior Struddell, wonderfully commoved. " And hath it thus come to pass ? Of a troth, an evil season, a time of trial and suffering is dawning upon our tribulated Church. In Mistress Boleyn's rise we must needs perceive our doom. She is fair and comely to view; but, alas ! she is one of Satan's most dangerous tools, and well hath she been named the she-Sampson of the accursed Lutheran faction. Alas ! what an evil chance hath happed in this matter ; for, peradventure, now will the malig-nant weeds of heresy grow thicker than ever aforetime, and for a while check the growth of the further harvestings of the good soil. But let be, let be! we must bear it, suffering all things uncomplainingly, until a brighter day redawns, when the folds of this heresy shall be utterly uprooted by fire and plough from all the broad surface of the kingdoms of this world."

"I say naught in malice or ill-will of thyself or thy convent, my lord prior. Withouten doubt thou mayest have been raised of God for the comfort and support of your, as ye term it, tribulated Church in these latter times. And, moreover, it may be, that by being thus exalted in your sanctity among the blackstoled brotherhood, like the solitary star of far-aloof brightness that directs man's barque across the trackless waters, thou shinest the brighter and nobler for the contrast with those heads of other religious houses, whose precepts and whose conduct are far from being akin."

"I am but such an one as the Great Author of the Universe created me, and I act in all things under His prescience as my conscience dictates. *Misericordia Domini eternam cantabo !*"

said the venerable monk, with a well-assorted admixture of dignity and humility.

" I crave pardon, my lord prior. I meant ye no offence ; for of a surety I would do thee a service an it be in my power, as witness the cause of my coming hither this eve, which let me apprize thee of without further wrangle. The King doth wish in all ways to pay homage to the Lady Anne's sovereign beauty, and would that ye of Blackfriars give a feast in her honour after the style and in accordance with the usages ye men of the cowl know so well how to simulate. And for this honour, my lord monk, you may certes feel beholden to me, who hath so arranged it. And let me, in furtherance of my goodwill on that score, avise thee to have thy feast and thy monkish disports of the best, so that thy house may find some favour with the new and rising light when the time of disruption comes."

" The King's wish is e'en a command. We will so unite our poor services as to give him and his court a worthy reception, as shall be proven. But on what day will the King that we receive his Majesty, to do him homage and lip-service within our exempt precincts," demanded the prior.

"On the eve, four days from hence, being the day after the general tournay, and the one ere the Lady Anne betakes herself to her lodgings within the Tower, previous to her departure the next morn for Greenwich, whence she sails it back again in gorgeous state and golden glitter, in earnest of her public coronation by Cranmer, his newly-made reverence of Canterbury," returned Cromwell.

"Short time hath surely sped, sith the King in the Court of Divorce yesterday proclaimed his stern will, to the carrying of it thus into impatient effect. And what hath betided our most gracious lady, Queen Catharine?" asked Prior Struddell, with re-awakened interest.

"The royal lady hath to Kimbolton, where she lies, they say, sick in body—and ill at ease, I no doubt trow," replied Cromwell.

"Noble lady, gracious queen! the worst of

whose ill-luck wert in mating thyself with
metal so false and base as this same bluff
Hal,—no king, I wot, either of right or deed,"
interposed Richard Plantagenet, vehemently.

" Odd's life, young sir ! be more chary of thy
ill-speech if thou would'st keep thy handsome
head on thy well-assorted body," exclaimed
Cromwell, with a reproving smile.

" But, despite the King's urgency, no measure
of divorce hath yet been perfected," exclaimed
the prior, interposing.

" Thou art in error, so deeming," answered
Cromwell, eagerly. " His Majesty hath more
than once I trow declared, that if peradventure
the lords legate failed in establishing the unlaw-
fulness of his yoke with Catharine of Arragon,
he would certes appeal to other judgment. This
hath he now done. My lord's grace, the Cardinal, compassing his own ruin, did yestre'en
declare somewhat too imperiously against the
King's most wistful determination, and as a
sequence his haughty and umbraged Majesty at
once appealed to Cranmer, who hath this morn,

by assent of certain of the bench of bishops, publicly declared his marriage with the Lady Catharine of Arragon void and of none effect."

"Alas! gentle lady, ill-starred queen, with thy misfortunes in thy regally banished state flee for a season the good hopes and peaceful well-being of the Catholic Church," exclaimed the prior, with considerable agitation.

"Be not cast down, revered father. The foundations of our Church, and of the great monastic institution, are too surely laid to be uprooted by the gusty storms thou seemest to discern foreshadowed in the future," exclaimed the young knight, with his usual impetuosity, while approaching the side of the venerable monk.

"All future events are in the hands of a Kingly Sovereign, who takes no counsel from earth or time. From that mighty fount hath ever gushed the inexhaustible current of religious zeal and fervour, which, from the early days of the great legislator of the Monks of the West—the noble, holy, and fearless St.

Benedict—hath ever shown itself impervious to all inimical assay amid our holy army of ccno-bites. But be thou patient, my son Richard, and walk upon the waves with the help of faith and obedience, being assured thou shalt find solid support amid the incoustancy of human things. For the rest, we must prepare ourselves to meet the coming storm as best we can. A punishment, we may be assured, will light on those heads who whirl it over us; for what other harvest, prithee Master Cromwell, should nightshade yield but its own poisonous berries? Your healings bear no panaceas on their wings, I trow."

" I will not discuss now, my lord prior, what is heresy with thee and saving doctrine with me. When it grows, and spreads its effulgent light broadcast over this land, then will I urge it more impressively upon thee, and then, mayhap, thou mayest espy some reasonableness in it. But I pretermit the cause of my wan-derings hitherward. Thou art avised of my messengery, and wilt nathedoubt have all thy festal gear in readiness betimes," said Cromwell, preparing to depart.

Ere he did so, the venerable prior signalled the knight of St. John to his side, and then whispered him, " Hist to thy ear, my son. Get thee gone with Master Cromwell, an he wants speech of thee; but come hither again anon. I have that to say to thee of no light import; meanwhile depart in peace."

The young knight thereupon proceeded forth with Cromwell, leaving Prior Struddell once more buried in the Phædo of the divine philosopher.

The sun had set, and the evening's mist was fast rising, subduing in its floating cobweb veils the bright glow of the golden twilight, ere they left the great cloister, and strolled forth into the convent close.

" And now, prithee Master Cromwell, wilt tell me the cause for which thou hast brought me hither, and required speech of me?" exclaimed Plantagenet impatiently, as he stopped and suddenly faced his companion. " I desire not forsooth, to be a mere page, in attendance at thy heels."

"Body o' me, how full of fire art thou, my matchless knight," said Cromwell, with a laugh; but, on observing a dark flush pass over the other's face, and an angry gleam in his eyes, he changed his tone, and added, "Look you, monk of St. John, I've ta'en a liking to you, and would not see you run so heedlessly into the lion's den as some, who are preparing to receive you, deem thou wilt."

"How mean you? I've replaced my broken sword, and who will venture to do me aught of evil?" demanded Plantagenet, drawing up his tall, well-knit form, and gazing with a fiery glance around, as if in expectance of some concealed onslaught.

"Peradventure none will essay thy life or thy liberty openly. Art thou not minded that dark deeds are best done secretly, and in the dark. 'Sdeath, mischief seldom lurketh about at noontide. I therefore bid you dismiss thy enthusiastic dreamings, descend for once and aye to real life, and beware how you give others you wot of further handle against you," said Cromwell, with impressive earnestness.

"Tush, Master Cromwell! What care I who frowns on what I utter, still less on what it beseems me to perform! Your scorpions will e'en bite themselves, an they try odds with me," responded the Knight of St. John, with haughty scorn.

"Howbeit remember that I bade you beware, and, when need shall be, that you have an assured friend in Thomas Cromwell. But let not thy obstinate courage be too flintily buried; for mayhap thou wilt sooner regret than thou deemest the non-observance of my warning. Thou art to joust on a day hence, with a certain high personage who hath saddled himself with the cause of the King, whom thou didst so roughly challenge. Take heed to run thy courses in silence, without further slip of thy unruly tongue, and in all wise conform to the strict law of tournay, else occasion will be found to set upon thee, and despatch thee to a long bondage within the Tower; or mayhap worse may befall, for thou mayest, on the spot, be done to death. Beware, therefore, of the madness of thy audacity; let it not forth, so that they who gaze sourly at thee may find fit occasion to bite as well as spit their spleen."

"How now, Master Cromwell? Thou speaketh with some hidden meaning, as one knowing more than he careth to disclose. Prithee utter your secret whisperings aloud to my ear, so that I may e'en be able to gauge their import and their worth."

"It is, as thou well magineth, not merely black shadows of suspicion that haunt me concerning thee," returned Cromwell, gazing carefully around, and through the numerous trees which thickly studded the greensward they lingered on. "You have enemies enow at court, I trow, and one who few have bearded on his throne, or done so and lived; but thou hast yet another, a cloven-footed one, I trow, in yon dark pile," pointing towards the monastery, "who, though toiling and sweating in the bondage of

a dotard monk, hath yet as much play of nature
in his veins as any among us, and is, moreover,
a fiendish espial upon all thy doings within
these precincts."

" Thou wouldst name Dan Theodulph, whose
glance but now darted such fierce though un-
uttered meanings. But let this false priest, an
it be so, beware of his nefarious projects ; for,
albeit he weareth the robe, and prayeth betimes,
he shall feel the scourge ere his felon purposes boast success," exclaimed Plantagenet,
with heaving breast and flashing eyes.

" Thou must needs be more chary of thy
speech, sir knight, and not rave so openly and
loudly as if thou wert urging on men in battle.
To let these wolves hear thy bleating wert surely
a needless vantage. Thou knowest not the black
carrion, which cry famish in these penticles of
monkery. But God helps him who helps himself. Go by my guidance, and thou mayest
stem the storm in safety, and baffle the malice
of yon beetle-browed sub-prior, whose look,
when thou art near, is much akin, I trow, to

cruddled vinegar. Thou wilt do well not to slight my counsel, and to look elsewhere than on the ever open portals of dreamland, and with that advice I now must needs depart."

They then separated after a frank and cordial leave-taking.

CHAPTER III.

The Abduction.

FOR many love-thralled minutes did the lovely Aveline sit entranced upon the soft couch where her devoted young knight had left her. She gazed out through the chequered casement of the noble chamber upon the darkening twilight of a Spring eve, as if her soul could behold those beauties of Nature and Nature's God which her resplendent but visionless orbs so intently lingered on. But heart, thought and feeling, like her sight, were not in the fair witching scene before her; they were away—away with him who had so lately left her—away, wandering in a fairy dreamland, in which no foul or leprous impressions had any association—away, building fancifully-pure erections of future glowing bliss upon the golden sands of love. Presently the light of the warm feeling faded from her seraphic countenance, while a something even of pale fear appeared to seize upon her; for she shuddered, and then, turning her head from side to side, listened intently, as if in expectation of some unseen and shadowy advance. The next moment however, Dame Agatha entered the room, while the voiceful notes of the vesper bird were heard without.

" Dear nurse, I would walk forth a little," she exclaimed on recognizing the footstep.

" Let us out then at once, for night is falling, and thou must not, sweet child, meet its shadows beyond these saving portals;" and the matron led her gentle charge on to the terrace, which they traversed to and fro, not venturing to wander in the gardens so late, since their late grave affrightment.

" Dost know, dear nurse, methinks my sight must needs be coming back again; for now that I face this way, it would seem I can discern, as if floating in a silvery mist, the farewell glory crimsoning the west. For the last few days, too, have I more than once fancied I could behold as in a dream the blue skies by day and the violet stars by night."

Laud be to our piteous Lady, who hath, perchance, heard at last my long prayerful entreaties so incessantly poured forth on your behalf!" exclaimed Dame Agatha in great joy.

" Ha! *Madonna mia!* It minds me well that Master Verstegans bid me not many days past to look speedily for a change, and that in the first redawning of blissful vision, I should have many daylight dreams passing before me like clouds in a fair sky, or the streaks of first daylight upon a darksome night."

"Ah! Jesu be. praised! For the love of mercy, Blissful Lady, grant this may come to pass!" exclaimed the dame in a rapturous ecstacy of joy and entreaty.

" *Sancta Maria!* permit me to behold once more the glories of creation; to watch the eternal sun, while rolling 'in the skies, gladden the earth ; to witness. the fleecy clouds whiten as they float beneath the moon; and to have these vague, undefinable mists, and shapeless forms transformed into real and substantial beauties. I fear to think of it, dear nurse; I dread to hope, while even at the blissful fancy my soul is shaken, and trembles like unto the sun's rays upon a broken stream."

"We will bide the issue, dear child, with no wanhope, sithence Master Verstegans hath avised thee of the yearnful change," said Dame Agatha.

"And if it so come to pass, I shall behold face to face him whom hitherto I have only imaged darkly in my soul," exclaimed Aveline, in a warm gush of that love which blazed from her soul, pure, sublimed, and impassioned as light itself.

"Oh, speak not of the youth, though well-favoured I wot he be; at least not after so warm a fashion! It is not comely; it is pernicious; nay, worse, it is adulterous to have such feelings alive in your soul, as Dan Theodulph hath oft afore this warned thee," exclaimed Dame Agatha with some asperity; for she was an eager disciple of the dark-browed monk, an ardent worshipper before the superstitious idols of Rome.

"I cannot command my thoughts, how much less my feelings, nurse Agatha. They will wander, despite my efforts to chain them; and what harm can hap through loving one whom instinct, as well as service done, bids me honour and cherish."

"The harm lies, dear child, in that you, a well-nigh plighted spouse of Heaven, nourish an earthly passion for a mortal born," returned the dame with somewhat stern emphasis.

"Speak no more after this fashion to me," said Aveline with rising colour albeit with easy dignity. "Thy words are those of Father Theodulph. I love Richard Plantagenet, and shall continue to do so, despite all contrary urgings, to the last day of my existence. In so resolving, I seek not to anger our Lady; and certes will I do all humanity can to redeem my soul of its impurity, but never with the intent of any longer fulfilling my plight and entering religion."

Dame Agatha stood momentarily aghast at this fixedly spoken resolve ; but quickly recovering from her surprise, she, more in obedience to the strict and earnest enjoinings of the sub-prior Dan Theodulph, than of her own more sympathetic promptings, poured forth into the not over-patient ear of Aveline a somewhat vehement diatribe concerning the heinousness of her resolve, and of the passions which prompted it. In the midst of her wordy reproaches, and even still more energetic advisings, the hour of seven tolled forth from the lofty belfry of the adjacent monastery, the sonorous sound whereof warned the worthy, though bigoted attendant, that night had already sufficiently sabled the fading glories of twilight, and that her well-loved charge had best be conducted, without further tarriance, within the sheltering walls of her dwelling-place. She therefore, stopping short in her somewhat vehement schooling, led the way to the ivy-covered porch of the terrace doorway, enjoining Aveline's quick following. As the latter turned in accedance, some unusual sounds smote upon her quick ear, and, for a moment, stayed her footsteps. She remained incapable of movement, with terror the most abject expressed in her face. She stood startled,—trembling like a frightened seraph beside her glittering bath, her long eyelashes pencilling her fair unspotted cheek, and shadowing the deep humid orbs beneath, like unto reeds skirting some translucent pool.

Before her fearful thoughts could find expression, or she could retreat from the unseen danger which made itself thus imperceptibly felt, the hired desecrators of her home-safety and virgin-peace were upon her, and with ruthless power, though with what gentleness such guilt-stained hands could show, seized her, and while covering her pouting, ruby-lipped mouth with a silken scarf to prevent an outcry, bore her quickly on down the terrace-steps, through the garden, and out into a quiet way of the Precincts, not altogether inaptly denominated " Hell Valley." Meanwhile, Dame Agatha, in the midst of her alarm and wild anxiety, shouted aloud for aid and the presence of some of the male servitors, who, pampered much after the same fashion as those who serve in high places at the present day, were comporting themselves too luxuriously to be easily disturbed, or quickly summoned. She also, with what strength she might, seized upon the martial habiliments of the most sluggish of the twin ravishers—no less hopeful a personage than Tony Vulp—and endeavoured to stay the mislawful abduction. But her efforts of voice and hand were of little avail; for Master Vulp, being quick in conception of villainy, was equally daring in execution, and stood not much upon ceremony in the handling of man or woman who crossed his purpose or barred his path. He therefore, while still aiding his companion Captain Roche, in bearing the almost unconscious Aveline forward, with a mighty oath struck round at the clinging dame, and very unmercifully felled her to the ground. Freed from this threatening obstacle, the twin worthies pursued their way, threading the varied intricacies of the Wilderness, and thwarting, with knavish instinct, all curious inquiry or semblance of interference. They at last reached, and without obstacle embarked from, the pier facing the hostelry of the 'Three Bells,' in a small barge whose oarsmen were seated in active readiness, and who immediately launched forth into the tidal waters, pulling sturdily up the river towards the steps jutting forth from the neighbouring sanctuary of Whitefriars known as " Alsatia." Here awaiting them was a small group with several led horses, the principal personage among whom, rushing down the slimy steps, aided in bearing forth from the boat the distraught and semi-conscious Aveline, and in lifting and securing her upon a large and comfortable pack-saddle, of the species then much in vogue among the wealthy and distinguished of the fair sex.

A glare, rather than a smile of satisfaction, lighted up the features of the swarthy Sir John Perrot, as he bid Captain Roche and his lieu-

tenant mount ; and himself seizing a led rein of
Aveline's horse, set the cavalcade in motion by
spurring forward up the rise of Water Lane,
leading through the heart of Whitefriars, whose
motley dwellers gazed upon the strangers with
many a querent and hostile glance ; but the late-
ness of the hour, the little commotion on the
part of these dubious intruders, and the absence
of all outcry for help and rescue, prevented any
hostile demonstration on the part of those who
were only too ready to uphold the great privi-
leges of their inviolate sanctuary. The sudden
onslaught, the rude hurrying onward, the fear
and dismay succeeding, for a while held the
gentle Aveline spell-bound to utter silence. And
when, by the sound of the iron footfalls of the
cavalcade, her quick sense of hearing distinguished they had left the teeming city behind
and were traversing some country roads, she
muffled her face and ears in her gauzy mantlet,
as if to shut out sound as well as light ; for to her
distraught feelings, and super-excited brain, it
seemed to portend naught but death and woe.

Her sweet spirit appeared sensitive as that refulgent flower of the sun which hides all glory when its life-giving lord withholds its radiance. Though confident in her own dazzling innocence, which, like the chalice of the Redeemer's blood, nothing impure or defiling had ever fouled, yet how fearful an ordeal had she to pass through amid the foul passions which, either secretly beneath some false cloak sufficiently delusive to cheat the fiend, or openly with determined passion and remorseless power, would assail her innocence and mayhap her girlish strength. But she grew gradually calmer as she was hurried through the moonlit air of night, and prayed very earnestly for that strength and aidance she, poor, timid fairling, so much needed. She trusted in the aid of her blissful Lady, and in the protection of the saints, without which, she felt, in her simple faith, that she and all else were lost and helpless.

CHAPTER IV.

The Alarm and the Pursuit.

THE robe of night had well-nigh cased the
earth, while the star-nailed heavens began
to glimmer with their myriad lamps, as Richard
Plantagenet, after his leave-taking with Cromwell, again wended his way towards the old
Manor House, with the intent of keeping watch
and ward over his lovely mistress's safety,
against the fell designs and evil happenings
of those who sought to prey upon her beauty
and her peace. He had reached the wicket, and
was about passing into the deeply-shadowed
gardens, when he was confronted by a tall,
dark figure in a monk's garb, whose voice the
next moment pronounced to be that of Dan
Theodulph.

"Whither away now, sir knight? Wouldst

seek the nest when the spoiler hath robbed it; or comest thou as knowing aught of Mistress More's whereabouts?" exclaimed the prior in an unusually excited tone, and in an observedly perturbed frame of mind.

" 'Tis a fair mock, mayhap, but let it be a plain one," retorted Plantagenet, with a haughty scoff. "Vouchsafe a meaning to your words, dan monk; for of a surety I espy none."

"Then thou art not of the inkle which hath wrought this wrong accursed; not one of these bloodthirsty ravishers, who e'en seek, after the fashion of Satan their master, to despoil ever the fairest blossoms earth's lilies shoot forth to light," exclaimed the sub-prior, breathing thickly beneath some suffocating emotion.

"Keep me not here babbling thus; but by the Holy Sepulchre, tell me, if thou canst, the real purport of your news!" exclaimed the Knight of St. John with fierce impatience, albeit a dread surmise quivered to the depth of his soul.

"Despite the jealous vigilance wherewithal I have haunted this chosen of Heaven, despite also the ounce-eyed guardianship of Dame Agatha, and despite too her own more tearful entreaties, certain thieves and swash-bucklers of incarnate hue have this eve—not so long since—burst in upon her home-privacy and borne her hence," said Dan Theodulph, struggling with all his mental supremacy to control the physical signs of an overpowering agitation.

"Borne her hence ! How, say you—borne her hence ! Mistress More, mean you ? How—when ? It is false—it is false, I say !" impetuously exclaimed Plantagenet, as he pushed the sub-prior from his path, and in an ecstacy of fear rushed towards the mansion.

As he entered the broad hall, the weeping and wailing of a female drew him into the banqueting-room, where, on the floor, enthralled in her grief and anguish, and with her dress awry through some evident rough-handling, lay Agatha, the devoted attendant upon his gentle love. To shake the ancient dame and rouse her from her tearful apathy, to pour upon her question after question, until the whole truth had been gained, and then again to rush forth and in his haste and savage earnestness to upset the sub-prior who had speeded in his wake, were to Richard Plantagenet the consequences of as many seconds. He then hastily summoned the various servitors, but none could give him any satisfactory information, or furnish a clue whither the despoilers had borne their young mistress. Without further loss of time, and still accompanied by Dan Theodulph, whose concernment seemed to equal, if not to surpass his own, the young Hospitaller enforced a strict search throughout the broad expanse of garden and shrubberies, but with, alas, the like futility. At last subdued by fear, dismay, love, passion, and revenge, he seated himself, as if too dizzy to stand, upon one of the broad steps of the terrace, and covered his face with his hands, endeavouring to bring his mind to dwell with something like calmness upon the outrage which had been perpetrated, and the steps most advisable for him to pursue. Now it was that the better trained temper of the

sub-prior stood the young warrior monk in
good stead; for drawing nigh, and gradually calm-
ing his own perturbed feelings, he addressed
the other, and with something of vehement
reproach in his tones.

" How comes it, knight, thou sittest here idle,
when thou shouldst be up and stirring, if thou
wouldst save Mistress More from pollution."

" Get hence, monk ! Get hence, I say ! I
have no tongue to answer thy gibing now," retorted Plantagenet fiercely.

" And so thou wilt e'en let an angel fall, ere
thou movest a step, or liftest an arm in her
defence !" persisted Dan Theodulph, and with
that searching look, which we sometimes encounter from those on whom the world has set
its mark.

" Art mad, to taunt me thus ?" cried Plantagenet, springing up, and fiercely clutching the
other's arm. " Dare not to anger me now ; lest,
by the mass, I forgot thy frock ! If thou hast
aught to tell me, speak, but be thou speedy. I
will to the rescue—but whither ? Not for all the

realms which the sun hath this night set on, would I linger a moment in seeking my gracious lady's succour; but whither—I say, dan monk, whither?"

"Here comes one, and with some speed, who perchance mayest tell you," said Dan Theodulph, as he pointed to the approaching form of the Maid of Kent, who, as she hurried up breathlessly, exclaimed,

"Away, away, sir knight; not a minute lose. The dovecot is empty, and the bird is in the hands of the fowler. They have ta'en water from the pier at the 'Three Bells,' and have from thence to Whitefriars, whither steeds of blood and speed will bear them to Richmond."

"Richmond!" exclaimed the Knight of St. John.

"Ay, of a surety. That much I learnt by following in their wake on hearing some womanish outcries of distress, and on perceiving a thickly garbed form, hurried along by armed men. Away, therefore, choose the best steed in

Master More's stables ; for of a surety, on such
an errand, thou mayest have thy pick, and take
with thee from among the menials or grooms-
men what aid thou deemest fit and mayest need."

Without heeding the latter suggestion,
Richard Plantagenet hurried to the stables
beside the ancient dwelling, and selected a
powerful and likely-looking horse.   While
tightening his own long sword, and borrowing a
dirk, it was quickly caparisoned.   As he placed
his foot in the stirrup, and vaulted into the
saddle, Elizabeth Barton again approached him.

" Be careful of thyself, dear knight," she
whispered, with tremulous earnestness. "Well,
thou must wot that atween life and death there
is not an instant. Take, therefore, heed to thy
own safety, in seeking that of hers you so
fathomlessly love; but let that thought also
strengthen your arm in any strife that may
ensue; for if you fall, the gentle Aveline will
have no protector, amid the serpent wiles which
even, if this danger be o'ercome, may yet be
thrown around her."

Without comment or further speech, the young knight burst forth from the thronged yard, heeding not Elizabeth Barton's enjoinings to take with him a sufficient force to overpower resistance, and buffeted his way through the narrow defiles of the Wilderness, whence, after some difficulty in obtaining the opening of the great fore-gate of the precincts, he put the good steed to its mettle, and sped across the causeway, and along the broad Strand to the village of Charing.

" Why help him to seek another, whom most thou wouldest have beside thee?" exclaimed Dan Theodulph to the Maid of Kent, after they had watched the young knight forth on his impetuous course, and with a sultry gleam in his eyes there was, as observed in the bright light of the newly-risen moon, no mistaking.

" And why should it trouble you so much, my lord monk, that this young girl hath been ta'en from your *fatherly* ministration?" said Elizabeth Barton with an answering taunt.

" Ha! wouldst slander me ? thou too—thou,

than whose false heart none other can reek up worse imaginings!" exclaimed Dan Theodulph, in a wild outburst.

"I confide naught longer in seeming virtue, or fair pretences," retorted Elizabeth Barton with deeper signification.

"What meaning am I to divine in thy words, thou woman fool, thou heretical Magdalen?" ejaculated the sub-prior with a terrible sneer.

"Have I not cause to know thee, thou traitherous monk; and from the first I perceived that it was an earthly, and not a heavenly passion, impelled you in your devoted interest towards the daughter of the newly-created Chancellor," answered Elizabeth Barton undismayedly.

"Ah thou!—what shall I term thee—thou womanly Judas."

"Go to monk, revile me not, for what art thou?—aye, answer me that; but what you are thou wilt of a troth remain, till thou standest on the threshold of the unfathomed gulfs of Hades."

"Oh! belie me as thou wilt thus secretly; but

prithee, Maid Barton, take heed how thou caballest of me when abroad. I have thee, Cyprian, more securely in my power than thou wottest. I have more evidence of thy heretical teachings than would suffice to fire a score of pyres, and Bishop Gardiner and his kin-folk Bonner, who have now the king's ear, have declared they will destroy all of the accursed Lutheran faction 'gainst whom cause of complaint and proof can be had," exclaimed Dan Theodulph in deep-bayed tones.

"Trumpet thy warning to the winds; they may bear it further than I, who heed it not," answered Elizabeth Barton with a scoff. "They with whom I am thought worthy to assort will never courage lose because, forsooth, such as thou gainsay us. We are all well amort that despair is far worse than revolution, and equally are we minded that we have to beat down the opposition of a rapacious priesthood before we can behold our blissful cause blossom as Eden in the first days of creation. But the same forceful conjunction of events which balanced

the eternal sun rolling in the skies, are propping
up this new Church of Christ; and will, in the
end, perfect the glorious superstructure. Therefore, let be, all the trials, all the throes, all the
blood, to be felt and shed in the Chrislian warfare now dawning; they will bear their fruit in
due season, and the curse of to-day will to-
morrow be changed into the eternal benediction
of history. This new-made bishop, this Gardiner,
so lately doctor of the canon law to the fallen
Cardinal, had best not meddle with the inevit-
able, lest peradventure he run and fall. Let
him, and such as him, be warned, that to
tamper with Destiny is to defy the gods, who,
in accordance with one of your superstitions,
never miss their revenge, while of a surety they
will incur the contempt of posterity, whose
benediction, after all, I trow, is the sweetest
element of glory, and the surest basis of
fame."

"Get thee gone, for a rank, and certes a
doomed heretic! Away from me, blasphemer!
Thy days be assured are already numbered, while

the few that are left thee shall be days of sorrow—that sorrow, too, which, by the cross of our Lord, is the most lasting of impressions, as the cypress is the most enduring of trees!" exclaimed the sub-prior in a dreamy, dizzy tone. "In the new idol thy passionate soul hath set up, count the hours of thy happiness even now past; for methinks, heart-bliss is not garnered twice in a life, albeit the roses of Pœstum blossom twice in a year."

"Farewell, my lord monk. I must to Master Verstegans' lodgings, for I would learn somewhat plainer whither turns the tide of events. Rest thou in peace, or, as thou wouldest say, *Benedicite!* What chance, think you, hath the Knight of St. John in safely rescuing his loved, but unmated wife; or what thou to school thy leprous treason again into her pure soul, if he doth?" and with a scornful laugh the Maid of Kent left him, and proceeded through the ancient gardens towards Baynard's Castle.

Dan Theodulph cast a strange furtive glance, full of some dire unfathomable meaning, towards her retreating figure; and then, while bending his steps with slow and thoughtful pace towards the monastery, he bethought himself of certain cogent circumstances after this fashion. " How chances it I stay my hand and give not this demirep of heresy to the flames? 'Tis a deciphered necessity; for is not heresy rampant throughout the whole moral fortresses of Christendom, and doth not the old love and reverence towards Mother Church perceptibly lessen. The great foundation, too, of all religious fervour and zeal—the monastic institution—hath been virulently assailed by the abased Cardinal, and is still more ruthlessly threatened by this spawn of Satan, Cromwell, as he styleth himself; while even a still worse portent is shown by observing how men's eyes are busied in seeking pretexts for the mischiefs they meditate against the shrines of the saints. It is not of a surety wise in me to spare one who is so great a blasphemer and heretic as this womanish nun. She threatens, too, and would e'en show her teeth. She would, too, thwart my plans concerning this sweet seraph, while in her hints but now she sought to fathom my designs. And this haught springald—this Plantagenet, will he have power to steal from me the reward of my long toil and danger—this beauteous Eve, whose shapefully twining arms would form an embrace no other mortal bliss methinks could compass. No—never; he shall die the rather, ay, perish upon the block, for his outspoken treasons, despite he cowers now within our sanctuary. No longer shall my blood rush so wildly in my veins; nor much longer will I allow the monk's garb to frown hourly on me like a curse for violated vows. No! I will possess myself of the wages of my past sufferings, remorse, and guilt. I will deliver up these twin espials on my free action, the one to the block, the other for the stake; and then will I cast aside these robes, so ill-befitting the warmth o my soul, and thus render my blissful doom more certainly assured. Ay, ay, sweetest Aveline, thou shalt away with me to other climes, to speed the rest of this barren and rocky shore of time, in mutual and continuous wooing, albeit the doing so wert to sink my soul fathoms deeper in the seas of sinful flames, and clog it with agonies eternal."

Thus disturbedly musing, he reached the private adit of the monks, leading from the . monastery to the sanctuary. Meanwhile, the young Knight of St. John speeded on his way. Better seat in the saddle, or lighter hand with the bridle, could no one have possessed. His noble steed—a powerful black charger—which, like himself, was full to overflowing of undaunted courage and fiery ardour, responded readily to all his inspiring urgings, and obeyed with wondrous instinct the slightest indication of his rider's impatient spirit. Fast sped they along the Strand—for such in reality was then the roadway so called—bordered as it was almost uninterruptedly by the laving waters of the placid and glassy river, passing on the right the many mansions and splendid inns of the nobility, and the immense market garden belonging to the wealthy community of Westminster Abbey;

for Covent Garden then brought forth in profuse abundance what now it only markets. He soon reached the verdant, woody, and picturesque village of Charing, consisting of a small inn and one or two rustic cottages, delightfully embedded amongst spreading trees and luxuriant shrubs, with its lofty cross marking the last halting-place of the remains of the beloved queen of the first Edward. Emerging from this through a delightful lane rising towards the great hay-market, where, during one day in the week, provender of the best was exposed for sale, he galloped on to the great Uxbridge road, which lay surrounded on either side by pleasant fields and prolific gardens, varied every now and again by a copse of dense shrubbery and undergrowth or a knoll well shaded by trees. A pure and cloudless sky, through which the moonbeams floated brilliantly, brooded over the whole district through which he careered with such eager speed; while something indescribably sweet, soothing, and caressing, appeared to breathe in the

balmy air, to coo in the wild notes of the
wood-pigeon, to murmur in the pigmy rivulets
which, at intervals, gushed across his road to
rustle amid the lofty leafed boughs of the
innumerable trees, and to flit past in the soft
breezes which ever and anon stirred the rich
pasture or seedlings of the many meadows.
On, on he sped, heedless of all save the goal he
sought; and while thus, with undrawn rein and
unpitying spur, he careered along his path,—

> " Fled past, on right and left, how fast !
> Each woodland grove and bower;
> On right and left fled past, how fast !
> Each cottage, hall, and tower.

CHAPTER V.

Old Richmond Palace.

SPURRING on swiftly, but silently, the cavalcade bearing Aveline from home and safety
to fear and dread unknown, tarried not on its
route save at the wayside hostelry pertaining to
the dwarf hamlet of Mortlake, where Sir John
Perrot dispensed with the further escort of Captain Roche and his lieutenant. He rewarded
them, however, munificently and to their perfect
satisfaction, bidding them, by way of farewell,
that in case of pursuit they should stay it at
all hazards, or give him speedy tidings at the
Palace. He then again spurred on with his
companions, and shortly after leaving Mortlake
plunged into the Old Park, which then stretched
along the river's bank a good mile or more in
width from Richmond Bridge to that of Putney,

containing within its limits certain beautiful and extensive Royal Gardens, now known as those of Kew, and a considerable dairy and grazing farm. An observatory, still in very active existence, as is well known, was subsequently, in the year 1769, erected in this park by Sir William Chambers.

The exact date of the original structure, on the site whereof stood that to which we wish to conduct our readers, is irretrievably lost in the vasty annals of antiquity. It is presumed to have been a gloomy old feudal fortress of some strength and considerable notoriety, and to have reared its embattled towers to the sky during the reign of Edward the Confessor. For though no mention of town, castle, or palace, is to be found in Domesday-book; yet in an ancient record of cotemporaneous date is to be traced a notice of the manor under its then title of Syenes, afterwards pronounced Shene, or Sheen —of Saxon nomenclature, signifying ' brightness and beauty.'

It is certain, however, that the site became

the property of the crown during the reign of
Edward I; for he with his successors, Edwards
II and III, possessed a palatial residence here,
in which the last-named monarch ended his days.
After the latter event, through many rolling
cycles of time, it pertained to the possessions of
the crown, or to some branch of the regal family
of this land, and has more than once been
honoured as the abode of royalty itself. Queen
Anne, the consort of Richard II, however,
dying here, worked so upon the sensitive feelings of the king, that he abandoned it, and
permitted the noble palace to fall into a very
ruinous state. It was, however, restored to
more than its former splendour by Henry V,
and in the year 1492 became the scene of a
grand tournament, held by Henry VII. During
the latter's reign, it was destroyed by fire, and
was thereupon again elaborately rebuilt and the
ancient designation thereof changed to Richmond—signifying the Ridgemont, or ' terraced
hill'—after the town of that name in Yorkshire,
from which the king had formerly received his

title of earl.   When Philip I, King of Spain, was shipwrecked, in 1506, upon the stubborn English coast, he was entertained here in great and munificent state by the same monarch, Henry VII, who likewise, seeking in it a sumptuous hospital during his last illness, expired within this palace in the year 1509.   The Emperor Charles V, of Germany, was lodged in this castle on his visit to England in 1523.   Here also was confined, by order of her sister Mary, the Princess Elizabeth, whose favourite residence it became after her accession to the throne, and where, indeed, she breathed her last, at the close of her long and glorious reign. In 1605, Henry, Prince of Wales, made it his chief residence ; while, in 1625, the courts of justice were removed from Westminster thither during the continuance of the scourging plague. In 1649 it was surveyed, together with the gardens and a portion of the old park, by order of Parliament, and in the year following sold; but shortly after the Restoration it again reverted to the crown, and was assigned as the residence of the Queen Mother for her life. Soon after her decease Vandalism laid upon it its blighting hand. It was dismantled, and subsequently pulled down, permission being granted to certain privileged persons, who were to hold their leases of the crown, to erect some stately mansions on the time and royally honoured site. The only relic left to chronicle this royal site is the entrance gateway to what was termed the Wardrobe Court, which may still be seen on one side of the green, having over its main arch the arms and supporters of Henry VII, sculptured in stone.

Speeding onward, along a magnificent turfy avenue, well and loftily arched on either side by gigantic trees — the leafy chroniclers of ages flown—Sir John Perrot and his party drew rein before the principal gateway of the palace. Seen thus near in the pale moonlight, its towers, gables, domes, windows, bell turrets, balconies, strange bartisans, and tiled roofs had a crude and strange aspect. The principal feature appeared to be that of excessive antiquity; for

many parts of the original structure still stood,
moulded into the more modern whole. The
discoloration of centuries had been, in some
places great ; for minute fungi overspread
certain portions, and hung in places in a fine
tangled webwork from the eaves and coping-
stones, while the mantling ivy, with massive
and gnarled branches, covered as it were with
an emerald shroud the remaining portion. No
part of the massive masonry which was exposed
to view had yet given way, though the large
stones were crumbling in places beneath the
searching and invincible hand of time.

There was an iciness, a fearful sinking, a
horrid foredeeming in the Lady Aveline's heart,
when she heard the hollow echoings ringing on
every side as the curbed steeds were brought
to a sudden halt within the paved yard. There
was, too, in her gentle thoughts an unredeemed
dreariness, which no goading of her proud and
courageous, albeit gentle spirit, could overcome.
She had not spoken throughout her fleeting
journey, judging rightly enow that to offer

expostulation, to use threats, or implore pity, were all alike useless, and would be but so many words cast forth to the winds. She was quick of thought, resolute of purpose, and not lacking in spirit,—though the almost unclouded existence she had hitherto passed through had offered no occasion for the display of either quality. This was the first essay wherein she had to face danger alone, and do battle for herself; and though her little heart mayhap beat somewhat quicker, and her cheeks wore a paler hue, yet, in the approaching imminency of her trial, her strength upheld her, and her courage failed not. She dismounted without offering resistance when oilily requested, and then bowed stiffly when welcomed by Sir John Perrot to the palace he for the time being called his own. But having done thus much tacitly, she naturally felt the time had come to protest against the outrage which had been done her, and to assert that she was no willing visitor to this her enforced abode. And this she did with a dignity and firmness which evidently had its effect upon, while it equally surprised, the bold man her capturer and his not amissly chosen companions. But Sir John was not one long or easily daunted; so, after rendering a profuse apology in very amorous language, he stepped forward to her side, and took her hand to lead her within the palace, but this she hastily withdrew, exclaiming the while—

" Are there no women servants within call who can attend me, or am I to imagine I am powerless in the hands of ruffians only ? "

" Call hither the chatelaine, and, gadzooks, be ye speedy!" shouted Sir John, to the castellain, who, with the male retainers, thronged the steps and arched doorway. " Your pardon, sweet lady; my actions are ruder than my thoughts."

" Spare your words, sir. You could not please me, with all the resources of your eloquence, nor justify the wrong you have done; for which, be assured, in good time you will have to render strict account, and be adjudged punishment," returned Aveline, with haughty impatience.

" The consequences of this my transcendant act I value no more, lady, than gamesters the pawn they play in sport ere they stake their gold. But, prithee, proceed and honour my poor palace with your presence. Yonder is the chatelaine, and the chill night air fans too rudely the velvet of your face," exclaimed Sir John, with a peculiar smile.

Aveline, without further comment or opposing, held forth her hand to the female servitor—a grave matronly dame, attired in a black satin robe and hood, nearly covered with prickled lace—who came forth with several serving maids, and with a reverential bend, to meet her. She then allowed herself to be forthwith conducted to the large hall or chamber of dais, wherein was laid a sumptuous banquet, or rere-supper—one which the gods might have left their nectar and ambrosia to share, and one which, whatever it lacked in genuine comfort, was certes made up for by rude and antique

splendour; while, upon the profusely apparelled
tables, brilliant sconces and chandeliers shed
their refulgent glare from the lofty roofed ceiling
above. But though the well-spread board furnished symptoms of comfort and splendour, the
large hall looked cheerless beneath its air of
deep and almost irredeemable gloom. The
windows were long, narrow, and pointed, and at
a considerable height from the dark oaken floor;
while from them feeble gleams of encrimsoned
light from the high moon without shed their
lack-lustre through the trellised panes upon the
dark draperies and antique furniture within. At
one side yawned a large fire-place, on the
mouldered lintel of which appeared the royal
crest and cypher of its refounder, Henry VII;
while within blazed and spluttered a large fire,
composed of mighty pine logs.

Preceded by a grey-headed seneschal, who
ushered them the way, the whole party, consisting, with Aveline, of Sir John Perrot, Sir Ralph
Sadler, the Earl of Pembroke, and the Lord
Percy, together with their grooms of the cham-

bers, and attendants, entered the great hall, and passing the larger or lower board, whereat all the attendants and servitors feasted, they proceeded to the orsille, as it was termed—a high table placed upon a raised platform, at the upper end of the hall, whereat, in general, the lord and his guests satisfied their stomach cravings. Upon this nobly spread table were many dishes, which have vanished from modern bills of fare, such as a lumber pie, with a thick wall of ornamental pastry, containing a strange admixture of divers game fowl, seasoning and forced-meat balls; soused gurnets floating in clary; a calvered salmon, a skirret pasty, a marrow pudding, various sallettings; roasted quails, a larded capon, together with many another epicurean dish; while among the numerous potations were a bowl of canary and malaga with a toast, a bottle of sack brewed by the pantler, goblets of malmsey, flagons of hydromel, wine-cups of hippocrass, measures of balmy metheglin, and pots of humming mead, besides a stone jar of strong waters.

CHAPTER VI.

𝔗𝔥𝔢 ℜ𝔢𝔯𝔢-𝔖𝔲𝔭𝔭𝔢𝔯.—𝔄 𝔇𝔞𝔯𝔨 𝔓𝔲𝔯𝔭𝔬𝔰𝔢.

SEATED thus against her will and inclination at the festal board, poor Aveline had to bear, as patiently as she might, the persistently repeated offers to partake of some of the many dishes and wines which were strewed in such profusion before her. But nothing, she was determined, should induce her to taste anything in such company, or until the rescue—which she prayed and longed for, and in her young enthusiastic nature fondly believed was now speeding after her—had arrived.

" By the faith of my body, lady, 'tis ill-luck to fast in the presence of a feast ! Why shouldst thou hesitate to quaff at the purple fountains of pleasure these luscious grape-juices foment in the brain and heart," exclaimed Sir John Perrot.

" I require naught from your enforced hospitality. So prithee, weary me no more with such fulsome offerings," retorted Aveline scornfully.

" Gad's life, lady, thou art sufficiently tart of speech !" said Sir John, with observable pique ; while his co-mates smiled in concert at his numerous assaults and timely rebuffs.

" We beseech your consideration for our worthy host, Mistress More ; he is not accustomed, we trow, to be so chided and opposed by one of your sex, among whom he hath ever shown himself a lordly peacock," said the Earl of Pembroke, with a laugh.

" He hath, moreover, proved himself a wondrous elixir to all love-yearning maidens ; and of a surety, lady, thou mightest go further and fare worse, notwithstanding his kaleidescope peccadilloes," added the Lord Percy, in the same tone of banter.

Aveline answered not, but besought she

might be conducted to a more privy chamber, and have some womanly tendance.

" Nay, lovely enchantress, depart not hence; for, methinks, in thy absence the very sun would cease to shine. By my faith ! Venus never yet eschewed the company of Ceres or Bacchus. Allow me to win your favour in all gentle acquiescence; for, as my boon friends here can avouch, I am not to be denied. It hath ever been my humour, and well it pleaseth me, to subdue a haughty and defying spirit to my will, as it doth the skilful rider to o'ermaster some steed of fiery mettle," said Perrot, with glowing warmth.

A vivid and bright expression of indignation instantly mantled the lovely face of Aveline, as she somewhat impetuously exclaimed, " Methinks I should abhor the very sun that shone on so disloyal and disgraced a knight as thou."

" Nay, anger not thyself, Aveline; for by my faith no force of circumstances shall take thee from me, now that I have thee within my own lodgment ! Nay, not all the treasures of earth should barter with me thy loveliness," exclaimed Perrot, in a voice of vehement tenderness.

"Exult not, false knight, in your fool's paradise of hope. Bethink thee, recreant noble, there are those who will exact, ere long, a strict account of speech, as well as act, done unto me," answered Aveline More, with undaunted warmth, while earnestly trusting in her bosom's fondest thought.

"Soh! fair one, thou shouldst have worn a lawyer's gown to make their dry and dismal science musical," said Sir Ralph Sadler, with amused interest.

"Thy words are as naught, sweet one, while thy presence shines upon us like lightning in a sultry sky," added Sir John Perrot, in a low fervid tone.

"Oh, that I had then the lightning's power to scorch as well as shine!" retorted Aveline with impatient scorn.

"'Tis but a sorry banquet, this which I had hoped to share with you in joyance, a feast

illumined by the sun of your charms among us,
beauteous Aveline," continued Perrot, with true
lover-like persistence.

" Keep me an enforced prisoner if thou wilt ;
but if thou art a man, let me hence to some
other secure tarriance, and bid me not answer
more of thy distasteful ravings by aught but
silence," said Aveline, with haught impatience,
though tears started in her eyes, despite all her
urgent efforts to suppress them.

" Be it so, gentle one, sithence thou wilt not
listen to the charmer, charm he never so wisely.
Ho, without there ! Bid the chatelaine hither !"
shouted Sir John Perrot, and, rising, he himself
conducted the fast-failing Aveline to the door of
the hall, where, with manifold demonstrations of
passionate concern and devotion, he bequeathed
her to the watchful custody of the elderly matron
she had before encountered.

The restraint her presence had imposed upon
the unruly gallants she so wistfully left was
quickly dissipated in her absence, and many
were the flowing bumpers imbibed, and more

numerous still the mutual jibes and taunts indulged in. But while thus flaunting Time in wild carousal, they forgot not the angelic innocence and beauty of their captive.

" What think you of my sweet gaol-bird? Is she fit object for a gentle recluse, or wilt she best shine my queenly mistress? Hers are no visionary charms, I trow. How say you, Pembroke, who art thought a judge on such matters?" exclaimed Sir John Perrot.

" I esteem her so beautiful a lady that Paris, methinks, must needs have preferred her to Helen, and bestowed on her the apple rather than on Cytherea," returned the Earl of Pembroke, with the warmth of genuine admiration. " Methinks I would to my grave with eagerness were her beauty to keep me loving company. She is one who seems full of Vesta's fires, and of a troth, Perrot, hath not shown thee many buddings of hope."

" By my father's beard, thou forgettest that woman wast created but for pleasure, as the passion flower merely for light, and thou shalt bear witness how deftly with a few honeyed speeches, and some ardent warmth, this dove soul wilt credit me and succumb! She will, mayhap, wail and rage at the onset, but gradually she will ruffle down like unto the sea after the tempest, when the sun bursts forth and illumines so brightly all its surroundings," retorted Sir John Perrot.

" Thou art, beausire, a deep Platonic, endeavouring, as ever you do, to attain the Eve of beauty and gaining naught but disappointment in all its forms. Thou oft bowest thy knee to the Baal of womanly beauty, but as oft loseth all comfortings," said the Lord Percy, tauntingly.

" The fiend carry thee for a ribald mocker! How callest thou success, if our last passage of arms hath been a disappointment! Have I not trapped, as well as sighed for, this new Eve, who, methinks, must outshine the first as the light of noon that of morn. I am well avised she is not a Paphian, but it needeth no long observation to see she is not a prude!" exclaimed Perrot, with a boisterous laugh.

" Of a surety we know thee to be the spright-
liest wooer of our sex, and we believe that even
Ovid might have studied something from thee,"
added the Lord Percy, in the same tone of
banter.

" 'Tis thy own envious longing that makes
thee so tart of speech," said Perrot. " Thou
must acknowledge, natheless, she will make a
most lovely light-o'-love. How say you, Sadler,
who art ever mine oracle ?"

" She is of sovereign beauty, certes, and
graceful, too, as Dian ; but I am well minded
that the poor lady little knoweth that 'tis our
most Christian wont to cast aside the flower
when we have blighted it with our nurture,"
answered Sir Ralph Sadler, with a covert sting.

" Why, gad's life !—what would the man ?
Surely the honour of our preference hath some
measure of reward in it," said Sir John, with
haught imperiousness. " Should our notice of
her affright all lovers ever after, deem you ?"

" I must needs confess, your grace, that the
woman whom I could love, must be pure in

deed as in name ; in name as in spirit ; in spirit
as the upmost summit of the snow-capped Alps.
You, a blooming and amorous cavalier, love to
glass your goodly form in woman's eyes, but
melikes not to behold gentle Purity disporting
herself in man's.   Your softly-nurtured captive
is not of the blood to brazen existence as a
light-o'-love, nor will she ever be brought to
your purpose by fair means or loving speech,"
said Sir Ralph Sadler, demurely, as one who
misliked the part he had already played in the
dread drama enacting.

"Thou art not altogether right in thy
reckoning, Ralph. She has turned as restive as
an uncurbed barb, I do acknowledge ; but what
of that ? She is not the witch of Endor, nor
has she the spirit of the hag of Ob. She is, I
trow, a flower to be gathered on a holiday ;
albeit there is risk that, in clasping it, one
fingers the devil's scorching hand instead. It
contents me well to see her as she is ; there is
more merit in the taming," said Perrot, with a
smile and an air of self-gratulation.

" By all mankinds ! I deem she bestows on your passion such frosty light as rather withers than nourishes the vine," added Sir Ralph Sadler, with a laugh, echoed by all save he on whom it fell.

" Patience, my friends. I pray thee patience yet awhile," retorted Sir John Perrot, with a flushing face and piqued heart. " It may so hap that my good angel, an I have one, will rule that in this love-strife I am not myself made fortune's idiot. I'll sun anew my heart in beauty's eyes, and within an hour's compass, call me boaster an ye like, if I return not to ye a well-treated lover of yonder bosoming maid."

" Gramercy ! good Sir John, ' man proposes, God disposes ; ' so the proverb rhymes, methinks," said Sadler, mockingly.

"Tut, man, never mock at the devil; so, prithee, give me none of your dismal forebodings. I know thee of old, Ralph, for as great a prater as the poet legend-monger, Messer Ariosto, who at present is the rage in

Rome, or as any other one of the men of lore or seers of our day. I dare be sworn, though you affect to be no judge of such ware, thou wouldst readily take my place and be the true Sir Launcelot, the fortunate knight of this venture!"

" God mend me! I hunger not after thy leavings, Perrot; though Mistress More is above thy ordinary ventures, and is one who may entice thee into deeper water than thou wottest. Why seek to meddle further in this matter? Is not one girl as like another for thy purposes as two poppies; why needs it thou shouldst cast a blasting mildew on so fair and gentle a lady? Take her hence; and, to avoid displeasant consequences in Blackfriars, hie thee to court with her as a fitting handmaiden to our newly-elected Queen, whose beauty she will, by the mass, outrival!" urged Sadler, with serious warmth.

" Nay, gad's life, that will I not! At court, forsooth! Why, she would have as many lovers burning themselves at her beauty as moths in lamp flames," answered Sir John Perrot, with a scoff.

"Hast forgot the young monk-knight, her champion? Think you he is not now spurring on to her aidance,—and, mayhap with good accompaniment,—to her rescue," insinuated Sir Ralph, with a smile.

"'Fore Heaven, let him come an he dare! Though, should he follow our scent, he is like to fall into the reach of an ambushed assassination, sithence Roche, unless he turn dunderheaded, bungling fool, will render good account of all who pass his way. But get hence with further mock, and bide here my return with what patience ye may. I will now in to visit my captive beauty, and perchance salute her more oft than once with a royal embrace, and ye know what that signifies. Mine be the guilt, mine the hell; for I am fairly enamoured of this coy nymph."

And so speaking, Sir John Perrot, with flaming visage, the effect of his fell feelings, or the more mazy fumes of the distilled grape juice,—arose from the table, and leaving his companions, bid them be of good cheer in his short absence, and then retired from the lofty festal chamber to seek that of poor, dismayed, gentle Aveline More.

CHAPTER VII.

𝔄 𝔗𝔢𝔪𝔭𝔢𝔰𝔱𝔲𝔬𝔲𝔰 𝔚𝔬𝔬𝔦𝔫𝔤.

THE chambers allotted to the beautiful captive, and to which, pale and trembling as a blanched winter leaf, she was conducted by the chatelaine, were on the first-floor, and faced partly the gliding river, and partly the well-wooded bounds of the old park. The first or ladies' boudoir was a somewhat gloomy chamber, large in its squareness and lofty withal, hung with tapestry, in which were unnumbered Cupids disporting themselves amid banks of flowers of every conceivable shape and hue, while from the skyey ceiling above Hymen and other Cupids showered flowers, as it were, on the dark oaken floor beneath. In one corner of this chamber, and built out within a small air-hung tower, was an alcove of later date, far

more rich and enlivening in detail and orna-
mentation. It was hung with gold-coloured
satin arras, rarely embroidered, and adorned
with dwarf-like figures of the Apostles and
Madonna; while in the far corner stood a small
marble altar, richly inlaid, surmounted by a
golden crucifix, and above which the arched
ceiling was wrought with an Aurora meeting
Night in exquisite artistic form and toning.
Beyond the boudoir lay the sleeping bower,
divided only from the former by a heavy silken
curtain. This was, certes, a very splendid apartment, and betrayed much costly taste in its
garniture and fittings. The hangings, the
chairs, and the couch, were of rose-coloured
velvet, fringed and embroidered with gold, while
all else was of corresponding richness. A lamp
in either chamber, the globes of which were of
rose-coloured glass, shed a warm soothing light
through the apartments ; while the uncurtained
windows of the bower chamber, looking forth
into the park, and displaying an ample
vista of a far stretching pastoral landscape,

admitted the gleaming beams of the high-riding moon. Several large vases, containing freshly-culled flowers, placed in the window recesses of the boudoir, gave forth an agreeable perfume; while on an inlaid oblong table were deposited clusters of the finest fruits at that early season procurable, together with some choice wines in antique crystal jugs. Such were the appointments selected for these chambers from fashion's gaudy world.

Thither, to this surface gorgeousness intended for her delectation and enthralment, the gentle Aveline, with heart untainted and form unmatched, was conducted. She had well and nobly faced her danger, while it stood in human guise before her, ably combated the depressing influences of her sexual timorousness; but now that she was away from her persecutors, by herself, with only one of her own sex in attendance, the revulsion came upon her, for a while palsying life and feeling. It could be seen she sighed, by the secret swell of her beautiful bosom; while from her ruby-lipped mouth a whisper, almost light as air, breathed forth the prayerful entreaty, "*Salve me, Jesu.*" She remembered little more until, awaking from her swoon, she found herself extended, propped up by perfumed cushions of rosy satin, on what, though undiscernible amid her eyes' eclipse, was a magnificent settle, with velvety appointments. At hand, carefully tending her, and ministering with womanly kindness and instinct to her revival, was the chatelaine, her only allowable attendant, who, when she perceived the warm life-blood spreading anew over the fair captive's face—a pale pinkiness gradually creeping over the snowy paleness, like flame on marble—did her utmost by words framed out of nothing warmer than female compassion, to soothe Aveline's perturbed imagination. In this, for a time, she did not over-well succeed.

"Pardon me, I am weak with fear," said Aveline at last, while melting into tears. "But prithee tell me, whither have they borne me, and with what object?"

"Thou art, lady, in Richmond Palace, brought

hither for what reason you too soon will know," replied the chatelaine gently, and with a mixture of compassion and admiration as she gazed on that reclining form and face, one of humanity's most perfect masterpieces, and one, too, in the richest flush of spring-time.

Ha, Madonna! Let me hold my breath and wake from this strange dream! And can such things be, while God's sun berays all darkness?" questioned Aveline, somewhat distractedly.

" If these old walls could speak, lady, many a strange and cruel tale of wrong, grief, and hate, would they chronicle forth," said her attendant, in a dismal tone. " But, good lack-a-daisy, it is not mine office to increase thy wanhope, I would rather do my best, an I could, to make thee reconciled to thy destiny, which, though not of the best for one of thy gentle nurture, may yet be flowery and meady amid gaudy state and gilded plenty."

The significance of this hint could not be mistaken by even the untutored worldliness of Aveline More, so she responded, and with more

firmness than her attendant anticipated. " For
what dark purpose seized in my home and
brought hither I conceive not, nor care I
further to know ; but naught that may hap shall
lead me to forfeit that celestial chastity and modesty of which our blissful Lady is the exemplar.
Moreover, I shall hold it an enforced devoir on
all good knights and true, to scout as felon,
false, and disloyal, he who hath wrought this
wrong on me. But I'll bide no further discourse
on such matters. There is a murmur in the
winds which heralds to my ears relief and rescue,
to another's judgment and punishment ; meanwhile, good my jailoress, wilt please you enliven
the hour and speed the time by relating some
of the weirdman's tales anent this old palace
and district, of which surely there must be many
afloat."

The chatelaine complied, and related some of
those tales of dire affrightment they whose science
needs darkness, terrific silence, and certain shelter from the espial of humanity mostly indulged
in—flavouring somewhat as they did of the old

illusions of the mediæval empirics. Nor were supernatural horrors lacking in the shape of ghostly appearances and warnings, odd sounds, and more fearful deeds, to give memorable interest to the ancient palace of Richmond and its surroundings, and which in their time rendered the ingle-hum of the nearest farm or hostelry, or the refectory of the Carthusian Monastery at Shene Vale, acceptable refuges after nightfall. More depth and pathos were given to these legendary recitals, by the baying of the watchdog and the owl's long cry heard without amid the rustling of the trees, and by the nigh approach of the witching midnight hour—that hour of calm delight to all thoughtful minds, when Nature appears instinct with secrets dark and dread; when a language is spoken around on all sides which he that sleepeth not may haply understand. Strangely impressive organs of commune hath the invisible world; dread converse doth it hold; fearful intercourse hath it with that venturesome mortal who would seek to pry into its mysteries.

Thus time, laden with Destiny, fleeted by, until the first hour of another day had in its newly-sped darkness, and amid the drowsiest silence, been proclaimed, when of a sudden a crashing peal of thunder reverberated throughout mid-heaven, that made the ancient palace tremble as if convulsed with ague, while the forked lightning blazed athwart the newly-descended pall of darkness spread without.

" Oh, blessed mother Mary!" involuntarily ejaculated the startled Aveline.

Amid the lull after the first concussion of the midnight storm, a heavy footstep sounded in the passage without, and, the arras being lifted, Sir John Perrot entered the boudoir, having, as we have shown fortified himself by excessive drink, to stifle in his selfish breast the horror of the wrong and cruelty he meditated. He beheld not to what he would reduce that bright, and as yet happy being, who, like a butterfly or an Indian bird, was reared alone for the sunshine and the most flowery paths of existence. He pictured not to his cruel sight, her morrow, when, robbed of her purity and innocence, and when, crushed like a lily beneath the coil of a snake, he cast her aside as nothing worth. His face was deeply flushed, and he had altogether the appearance of one disturbed in some heavy wassail. He was, indeed, handsomely tired in a changed costume, that consisted of a doublet of white cut velvet roped with pearls which fitted his thick, well-knit form to admiration, and of hose of white satin slashed with the palest pink, while many a rare gem sparked in the massive ornaments wherewithal he had graced his person.

When Aveline heard his footsteps—for with the wondrous instinct Providence hath bestowed on the blind, she at once recognized them—a scarlet tint instantly o'ermantled her blooming complexion, succeeded as speedily by a waxen paleness. She, however, quickly recovered her composure, and as the chatelaine left the chamber at the command of her haught master, she prepared herself to withstand the stormy surge of Passion.

" It gladdens me, my beauteous captive, to
see thou dost not treat my efforts at thy comfort after the fashion which too many of thy
glorious sex are wont to do, with weeping and
wailing—dumps and dolours. Thou wilt find
this, so soon as thou art customed to thy loving
bondage, a gay place, and merry withal. But,
prithee avise me, sweet dulcibelle, what thou
lackest for thy best comfort?" demanded Sir
John, with warm eagerness.

" I seek and require naught within these
walls save thy absence," answered Aveline, with
easy dignity, though a flush of indignation
had o'erspread her face at the warmth of his
language.

" Nay, nay, dear Aveline ! Be not so harsh
of tongue to my sincere devotion. Why, of a
surety, thou wouldst not merit being ducked
on a cuckstool for a scold !" said he, as he
approached and seated himself beside her on
the well-stuffed settle.

" What manner of man art thou, to weary
and insult a lady after this fashion ?" demanded

Aveline, with scornful fury in her lustrous orbs.

" By the holy Paul, I scarce can tell ye, what manner of flesh and blood I am ; for of a troth it misgives me if I am so far self-taught !" answered the mad-cap noble, with a laugh. " But of this I can assure you, gentle demoiselle, there is no philtre—albeit my veins appear to flow only fire—but thy divinest and most subtle spells of beauty ravaging my soul. I can but henceforth live thy slave and die thy bonds-man."

" Speak no more of this, or if you do, I will not listen. Go hence, and leave me, if you have aught of knightly grace within ye. In our Lady's name go, and insult me no further, unless you wish to have the perpetual remem-brance of my scorn twined like serpents amid your heart-strings," urged Aveline, in tones which vibrated through the passion-tossed soul of the unbashful noble, though it added but fresh fuel to its sultry fires.

" Howe'er thou prattlest, ever dost thou melt

language into music; and methinks I hear a
seraph warbling; while about thee, of a surety,
revels seemingly the very air of Paradise. By
the mass, I do believe thee to be some fairy
Venus, come to me from thy native heaven!"
said the amorous Perrot.

"What mean you by such converse, my lord,
for such I am induced to believe you? Seek ye
my hand?—if so, I tell you on the moment, 'tis no
more mine to give; and moreover learn, for your
disloyal conduct, that I would never, did this
world contain no other of manly form than
thou, mingle the purple of my blood with so
contaminate a stream as thine," urged Aveline,
with indignant impetuosity.

"Oh, let not words so bitter flow from lips
whose roses blossom such blissful fire," passionately retorted Sir John. "Canst thou not,
sweet one, apprehend a reason for that passion
which possesses me, and which, by my faith, no
torrent can quench?"

"I wish not to know aught concerning thee
or thy feelings. It suffices me that I recognise

in thee but too well one about whom there are, certes, whispers, universal as the wind, discoursed most unmeasuredly. In me your brutish excesses of love infuse only indignation and loathing. Take to thy assurance that thy foul passions can kindle no answering flame in any but hearts as sulphuric as thine own," urged Aveline, withdrawing from the close contamination, the lawless contact, and lewd grasp, the unruly noble sought.

"Nay, thou dost me grievous wrong, lady mine. I swear to you by all the saints above the golden stars, I seek thee with a fever mine heart hath never aforetime known, and I can not conceive it to be in your womanly humanity to resist the wondrous allurements I can offer thee. My heart, my dreams, my hopes, are all thine, and before thee I kneel to the glowing shrine of love. Oh, be thou mine, sweet seraph, and I will bestow on thee more gems than hang on a rosebud at dawn!" he exclaimed with impetuous ardour.

"Blessed Virgin! O holy Mary! hear this

man's false leasings, and teach him them to his
utter berayment. I tell thee, sir knight, an
thou art one, which my mind misgives me, I
despise thee, and loathe thy ungenial attentions," said she impatiently.

"Teach me then how to woo thee, young
celestial. I am no Damon your charms to re-
hearse, but of a verity your beauty entrances me
and makes me but a child of ardent passion,"
persisted Perrot, with increased ardour.

"Dost mind thee that I have already told
thee I love another, and am to him betrothed,"
answered Aveline vehemently.

"Oh, in very troth, I forget it not, sweet
dulcibelle. But of what avail, gad's-my-life, is
thy liking for this boy-knight of St. John,
sithence he is, I trow, almost a priest?" retorted
her companion.

" Thou canst not fool me after that fashion.
The knights of the Holy Sepulchre, even when
shriven to their august monastic calling, are at
liberty, I well wot, under certain restrictions, to
ally themselves with our sex, how much more

then may he who is as yet but a neophyte amid their knight-holy company," said the lovely girl with a smile of ineffable disdain.

"Thou art a modern Plato, so well thou reasonest. But bide thee, bonnibelle, while I show what love, of which thou canst but little know, really is." And, thereupon, Sir John Perrot discoursed somewhat at length upon the great and subtle fire, urging certain definitions, at the spiritual subtlety of some of which Plato himself might have been puzzled, whil e certes, at the material glow of others, Sappho would no doubt have blushed.

Poor Aveline was beside herself, and knew not what to do, the white satin of her skin suffusing all over with a pinky tinge, while she answered him by way of comment, and while cowering down like a hare when the hounds are upon it—"Thou cruel man; thy own dark purpose makes thee bold to utter such words in my hearing. What thinkest thou of thyself, —thou who hast by thy deeds so falsified nature's bright mintage, man? I am, however, no

sphynx to understand thine enigmas, nor seek
I, as our blessed Lady is witness, to learn
further their meaning."

"A home, a world, a paradise I have found
in thee, so, prithee, chide on, thou loveliest—
by the mass for my part, I will kiss!" exclaimed Perrot, with impetuous fervour, while
endeavouring to encircle her fairy waist with
his arm.

"O Madonna!" exclaimed Aveline, wildly.
"Have I fallen so low that I must needs become
the sport of a ruffian noble?" and she sprang
from the settle and retreated a step like a
haughty Juno.

The attitude that in her palsied indignation
she assumed, appeared only a new variation of
beauty; at least so thought the enamoured
Perrot, as he viewed with the eye of a con-
noisseur the graceful contour into which her
gesturing threw her head and pliant form,—a
posture which Phidias himself might have
imitated. He arose, and, ere she could again
escape him, seized one fairy hand in a grasp

which all her struggling could not free, and
then kneeling at her feet, poured forth his ex-
cuses in a most lover-like and dulcet tone.

"Oh, in our Holy Mother's name, forbear!"
cried Aveline, in the sudden bewilderment of
fear.

"It is not in human nature to resist thy
loveliness. By the blessed stars, whose brightness thine own outrival, I cannot! Thou must
not, gentle one, longer waste thy beauty and
the loving hours of thy youth in the dim
obscurity and foul odours of Blackfriars, or
beneath the hoary tutelage of those pucker-
browed monks. Nay, thou art in wholesome
thraldom here, an thou wouldst be reconciled to
it; and here shalt thou tarry, and be hence-
forward the sole talisman of my power and
glory—my Aurora's ray and my Cynthia's light."

"*Thou!* What art *thou* to me?" and she
snatched away her hand, while the tempestuous
heavings of her full bosom too plainly attested
the fire of indignation raging within.

"Medoubts, my proud one, which melikes
best, your plaintive coyness or your queenly

anger. But thou shalt not brave me altogether, lady. Mine thou shalt be, I swear, if all the fiends of hell were matched against me. But so well do I love thee, so greatly adore thy pearly beauty, that, by the rood, I offer thee on the instant my hand and heart to share with me as my incomparable wife the rough-hewn path of my future life! How say you, lovely Aveline, wilt have me for thy mate?—ha!"

Aveline's pride, which never for a moment deserted her, at once, though somewhat inconsiderately, impelled denial. Her splendid eyes filled with fire, she grew very pale beneath the potency of her outraged modesty, while her beautiful mouth expressed all the scorn and anger that swelled up in her breast, as she vehemently answered: " St. Mary!—I know not whether to weep with anger, or laugh at thee in scorn! Mate with so disloyal a knight as thou?—never —never, though by the denial the next moment were my last! Art answered man, or needeth thy knavishness and hypocrite's wiles still further scorn and refusal?"

"Rash girl!—thou shalt not brave me thus heedlessly. There is but one way left to reason with thee. Bethink thee I am a child, a boy, a fool, to be trifled with thus?" he exclaimed, as he again seized her and this time encircled her waist with his well-muscled arm. "Nay, do not shudder or meditate aught frantical, thou fairest but most inanimate of all Eve's daughters, for I swear to you by all the four blessed gospels, thou shalt not 'scape me now, no matter what the consequences that may ensue!"

"O, Mary!—blessed mother of compassion, help me!" piteously exclaimed the distraught girl, as she vainly attempted to glide from his ruthless arms.

"Nay, weary not thy nightingale voice in such fruitless outcries. Thou art, sweet one, wholly in my power here, as an we were in a desert; and, by my troth, 'twere as impossible to have avoided this embrace as to clasp the plague till it were rotten and share not the foul contagion!" answered Sir John Perrot, with a flaming visage and with passionate fervour.

" Mercy, mercy! O holy Jesu, blessed Mary, help—help!" was the piteous wailing cry borne forth in despairing accents through the ancient palace, and forth through the casements into the murky storm mist and the deep blue noon of night.

Richard Plantagenet, young, lion-hearted Knight of St. John! Sun of chivalry! Why tarriest thou in thy coming ; why dalliest thy urgent rescue? Hark! 'tis the voice of thy beloved, thy betrothed, that vainly sues for mercy—that calls aloud for aidance which tarrieth too long.

CHAPTER VIII.

The Pursuit.—A Hindrance.—A Bed of Nettles.

THE speed at which Richard Plantagenet held on his way in his eager pursuit, soon left the metropolis far behind him. Along the solitary road, through a country of pastoral tranquillity, broadcast over which Ceres appeared to have shaken her horn of plenty, and amid the night-hum, the sound of his horse's clattering hoofs alone broke the death-like stillness, awaking echoes from afar. He passed none from whom he could glean information of his chase; and his mind became, each onward stride, more and more a prey to fear and apprehension. He kept his eye fixed on the seemingly interminable straights and windings of the road, but no trace could he discover of those of whom he was in pursuit. Through Chelsea marshes, across the ferry at the reach above, where he had some trouble in rousing the lazy Charon; across Putney Heath, of which a large portion was then a stagnant marsh, where the tree-frog and the bull-frog croaked in chorus so dissonant, as to challenge Aristophanes to produce sounds in imitation; over Barnes Common, where the ceaseless cry of that most indefatigable and restless of night-farers, the whip-poor-will, sounded shrilly in the moonlit air; through Shene Vale, amid the green glister of lizards darting out of their ferny coverts, and the shrill cries of some wandering moor-fowl, he careered along, and at last reaching Mortlake flats, drew rein before an hostelry which afforded for those primeval days good ' up-putting' for man and beast, and whereon the silver moon shone with a light like that of a rayless sun. He watered his panting steed at the long wayside trough and called aloud for the hosteler; for it was not much past curfew, and the swing-door in the porch still stood open.

The ancient hostel was of quaint aspect, but prettily situated in a wild and legendary spot.

It was almost completely overshadowed by a gigantic oak-tree, on one of the lower branches of which swung its signboard, and under the shadow whereof were placed a rough-hewn table and some benches for the accommodation of those customers who preferred open-air entertainment.

While the fat, loquacious, good-hearted, and ignorant Boniface came forth to do his customer's bidding, there was a sudden whispering beside an archway which led into the yard and stables adjoining, between two sturdy knight-errants who had been the moment before carefully tending their smoking steeds.

" 'Tis the Knight of the Sepulchre, curse me!" said one.

" I would cross him an I dared, but 'sdeath an I did so in this thwart light, he will certes detect me as plainly as the sun in an eclipse," said the other.

" By all my sins, 'tis he! See, he turns this way, while he inquireth somewhat of mine host!" said the first speaker.

" Od'slife ! we must stop him at all hazards. Hark'ee, Vulp, do you take a wide berth and circumvent him on the further side, while I approach him on this ; and as he stoops to reach yon goblet mine host is preparing to bring him, we will unhorse and secure him," said Captain Roche, for he it was, as the reader may have imagined.

" I'd as lief crack his skull as an egg," suggested Tony Vulp, in a thick gutteral voice.

Nay, dolt, that must not be ; leastways, till we have learnt his errand ! There may be more on the same track ; for, gadzooks, this young cat-a-mountain would hardly venture on so rash a deed as to come alone and on so delicate an errand —such a vagary would be unbefitting even a knight of the Round-table," urged Captain Roche.

They at once proceeded to put their design into execution, and ere the surprised Planta-genet could strike a blow or give rein to his fiery steed, they had succeeded. He was seized in vice-like grasps, dismounted and disarmed.

He, however, struggled hard, and with a strength
and energy which gave the pair of knaves more
trouble, and cost them a greater waste of breath,
than they had at first imaged.

" Whence comest thou, and whither going?"
demanded Captain Roche, pantingly, after he
had strapped with painful taughtness both the
arms and legs of their now helpless captive.

" Dogs of hell, release me, or I will give thee
such short shrift as ensues between the lifting
of my sword and the cleaving of thy felon
skulls!" wildly shouted the Hospitaller, the
desperate thoughts, this unforeseen mishap had
excited, gleaming madly in his eyes.

" Thou art a winsome youth and gallant, but
ere an hour be spanned thou mayest need the
best of thy mail and thy manhood to boot. So,
'sdeath! keep thy tongue in thy mouth," said
Captain Roche, with a dark, sinister look.

The Knight of St. John had ceased to struggle,
but his labouring breast still evidenced the strife
within. He thought it best to speak his capturers more fairly, and offered them a sum in
gold as black mail.

"Thankee! but, curse me, it wont do this time! I am minded of the saying, 'Ill-come is never well-come,' and thy gold as a bargain for thy release wert not an unlikely exchange for a halter or a poniard. He whom I now serve is not apt to bless those who miscarry his plans; and though I am not one to nurse fear in my brain-pan, yet, od'slife, I am inclined to fancy 'tis worth staying in this world as long as one can, were it only to keep out of the next! But let us in. I am as ravenous as a hawk, and mine host hath got a supper ready, which might satisfy the greatest epicurean, an he had fasted two days and galloped one."

Forthwith seizing the almost helpless Plantagenet, Captain Roche, in his steel cuirass and gorget, his hanging sleeves and long black riding boots, with sword, poniard, and pistolette, strode forward, and entered the ancient inn, mine host, in sore amaze, and amid some dubious shakings of the head and voiceless mutterings, bringing up the rear.

The hostel at Mortlake contained one large rude hall or apartment, where all visitors, with-

out any regard to sex or rank, partook of
refreshments, and were accommodated for that
purpose with plain and sturdy tables of oak.
The host having come to some satisfactory con-
clusion with his conscience, now bustled about,
and, while performing multifarious duties, talked
incessantly, even when blowing, through a reed,
the fire in the deep-arched fireplace at the
upper end. He chiefly descanted on the oft-
repeated praises of his numerous customers,
diversifying his converse, however, by eulogiums
of no mean import on the viands which he was
preparing, and forthwith proceeded to lay out
on the nighest table. These consisted, among
other dainties, of a pasty of pouts (moorfowl),
dishes of salmon, caught in the river close by,
cooked many ways, a larded capon stuffed with
forcemeat, and a pudding of plums and spices;
while goodly flasks of Canary, Rochelle, and
Bordeaux, reared their necks amid the numerous
surroundings. Captain Roche having deposited
his captive on a bench beside him, set to work,
in company with his well-attuned lieutenant,

and with an appetite which promised to cry havoc amid the good cheer provided.

" Now, Gad's my life ! I care not to stuff my stomach-void full of these dainties, and see thee hard-pinched with the cravings of thine ! So, an thou wilt pledge me thy word, Sir Knight of St. John, not to attempt a release of thyself from our bondage, I have just bethought me that I will e'en take thy pledge, and unfetter thy limbs. How say you, is it a bargain struck, or nay ?" exclaimed Captain Roche, as he buried his red nose in the wine pot.

" Release me an ye will, but no such pledge will ye have from me," answered the young Hospitaller with haught impatience ; but then, as his thoughts reverted to Aveline, her danger, and this most dire delay, he again tested his capturers with the potent argument of a golden ransom.

" Of that anon. 'Sdeath, 'tis out of fashion for conscience to cheat a man of reward ! So look ye, sir traveller, and for thy comfort be it spoken, I tell thee now, that I have a project

which hath certes just been put into my head,"
said Captain Roche, rather unsteadily, for
already his frequent visitations to the wine-pot
were beginning to take effect.

" By whom ?" questioned Tony Vulp, looking
up for the first time, and resting awhile in the
midst of his gorging.

" The devil nathedoubt, who, as thou wottest,
Tony, never lies dead in the ditch," answered
Roche with a full-mouthed oath.

" And of what colour is thy project?" in-
quired the Knight of St. John, with notable
impatience.

" Be not chafed, sir knight, nor o'er impatient. I must bide my time. Host of mine,
faith thou swellest and wallowest amid the good
things of this life, an ye live always after this
fashion," said Captain Roche leisurely, while
looking askance at Plantagenet. " But methinks, young sir, thou art too freely gifted with
the power of comporting thyself easily under
displeasant circumstances ; so, an it please ye,
we'll postpone yet awhile—perchance until the

morrow—what further may be said on the matter of thy ransom."

" Nay, hell-dog ! It must be this night, this hour, without loss of further time, if thou wouldst profit by thy knavishness," wildly shouted Plantagenet, while he vainly strove to burst his bonds asunder.

" God's murrain! Keep thy tongue in thy teeth, an thou wouldst have soul and body hang together. Thou mayest ride a horse like the demon of the wind, but thou canst not burst forth from hence until I bid thee," said Captain Roche, a dark frown spreading over his fierce brow.

" 'Sblood, a blow from my poniard, or a bowshot at fifty paces from yonder hanging implement would silence such scurviness, and were a fitter rescript, captain, than all thy homilies !" urged Tony Vulp, in a hoarse whisper.

" Out on thee for a fool ! Thou knowest not what thou pratest; leave me to deal with this fiery youngster. I want none of thy schooling," said Captain Roche, and then turning to the

Hospitaller once more, he added, while lifting a brimmed flagon of Bordeaux to his lips, " I heartily pledge you a speedy release, reverend knight," and emptied the vessel with a quaff which appeared to threaten his own survival.

" But what hath happened the man, for, beshrew me, thou art of as many tints as a vineyard in October," observed Roche, after a short pause, as he looked at his captive, whose fiery spirit and proud heart became daunted when he thought of his lost and hapless Aveline. It seemed as if some exquisite strain of harmony had suddenly ceased to vibrate on his senses, some fairy light become extinguished on his path, some delicious essence had been robbed of its airy fragrance, in the thus enforced and dangerous absence of his young and beauteous love. But he answered not the inquiry of his capturer, who, however, continued, either heedless of the torture he inflicted, or desirous of harping upon the same string, much as the cat plays with its feathered doomster—" By the mass, thou lookest as whey-faced as an thou hadst been listening to some tale, sad as a grandmother's when a fox hath been rifling her hen-roost!"

" Go to, swashbuckler! I value not thy gibes a rush," shouted the young knight, with sudden fierceness.

" Now, may the devil burn me, thou art sore anent the capture of thy light-o'-love! And well thou mayest; for foul fall me if ever I beheld a prettier piece of flesh and blood! By the mass, she is of sufficient pearliness to convert the fiends in hell! She is, I trow, in dangerous keeping: for, mark thee, her jailor is not only a man of substance, but is, certes, as wise as Nestor and as cunning as Ulysses," exclaimed Captain Roche, in a taunting tone.

" Dog of a villain, keep thy false fustian speech for thy own enlightenment! Give me freedom but for one hour, and I will, on my honour and knighthood, back to thee, meanwhile having rendered such account of he of whom thou speakest as to require naught further for him but a shroud for his foul body, and masses for his recreant soul. Take then my plight, and give me again my arms, my steed, and this furlough, and thou shalt have thine own guerdon," urged Richard Plantagenet, with earnest vehemence.

"By the rood, no! It is impossible. A pyramid of gold couldst not bribe me to it. But set thy mind at rest; thy mistress is in good keeping, I warrant, and, ere Luna's hour wane, will be reconciled to her state," said Roche, with a coarse laugh, echoed more lustily by his muddled comrade.

Plantagenet answered not save by a glance, which, in its fierce intenseness, spoke more than words.

"Od'slife 'tis useless to starve thy body, albeit thy mind seems so crustily adry! Wilt have a pull of this Bordeaux? 'Tis good drinking I do avouch. Come, have patience, sir knight I pray thee, patience, and to drink while you are able—for I reckon no man drinks for ever, nor can he fill his cup from every brook with such vinish nectar as this. What!—still pigheaded. Of a troth, I deem ye one of those that naught will persuade out of their determinations, which ever seem nailed in their minds like bad coins on a Jew's change-table. Well, well, by all the furies, if thou art inclined for churlish sociality, thou shalt have thy fill of it, and a pest on thee for a canker-bitten churl!" said Captain Roche, and turning away in sottish umbrage, he drew an armed settle towards the arched fire-place, and called aloud for more wine, which, for some reasons best known to himself, the worthy host took care most amply to supply him with.

Ho! drawer—Cyprian, I say! More wine, more wine, knave, and of the best," shouted Tony Vulp, by way of seconding his superior's command.

" Ay, ay, by the mass, more wine now, that we may not be interrupted hereafter!" echoed Captain Roche, unsteadily.

" Have ye not had enow, good my guests?" urged the hosteler, knowing the suggestion would only act as a powerful incentive to further carousing, and giving, at the same moment, the young Hospitaller a look of peculiar significance, that intimated intelligibly enough he was bent on some friendly project.

" Bah ! Deem you, mine host, I am a hermit, or that I have need of attempting to resemble old Anthony of Padua ? So, 'sdeath, bring up thy wine, or my fellow here shall visit thy cellar, and rifle it of thy best !" shouted Captain Roche, while unbuttoning his doublet and gorget, and incautiously flinging aside his sword belt with its weapons attached.

Tony Vulp imitated his leader's example, and, having relieved himself of his weighty garniture, drew in towards the fire, for the large hall was chill in the night air. He was evidently fast approaching that nimble state of semi-intoxication which inflates the head, warms the heart, lifts up the curtain of the inward man, and sets the tongue flying, or, perchance, tripping in the double sense of nimbleness and titubancy.

" 'Sblood ! my stomach is weak, and I am, by all the furies ! somewhat subject to dizziness in the head. My memory, mayhap, is not altogether such as it was; and, moreover, my faculties of attention seem in a measure impaired," he muttered, in a drawling, uncertain tone.

"Devil burn you, but, Tony, thou art very drunk!" cried Captain Roche, as he unsteadily reared another flagon of the newly-furnished wine to his coarse, sensual lips.

"By the body o' Bacchus, thou art no better than a horned owl to say so!" retorted Vulp, with a sottish scowl.

Meanwhile the Knight of St. John sat apart, almost unnoticed, his arms and legs smarting painfully beneath the taughtness of their leather swathements. He had seemingly grown callous to all external objects, absorbed in his own heart-corroding fancies, revolving and re-revolving in his mind this accursed mischance and its direful consequences, at last becoming a prey to the most exquisite torture. He beheld himself—the lone descendant of the haughtiest and noblest line of kings, wooed by few of the delights of existence, yet a sworn soldier of the cross, a warrior, too, of no mean pretence, full of noble daring and all-lawful ambition—thus time-locked and incapacitated from lifting hand or wielding sword in the defence of his gentle, loving, but helpless mistress. The mad whirl of his thoughts grew each moment more and more past all human abiding, and his smothered passions began, like the fiery draft of a fresh-lighted furnace, to surge up into the fiercest rage.

He was of a sudden startled by finding the strapping round his feet released, and hearing the bustling landlord trip nimbly away to another part of the chamber, directly fronting him, where, with his fat cheeks richly tinted with the colours of the grape, he smiled, and made the knight a sign of silence and caution. Meanwhile the two worthies continued their carousal, imbibing flagon after flagon of the purple grape juice, and gradually getting each moment more and more incapable of thought, observation, or action. Scarce five minutes more had elapsed ere Plantagenet heard a slight jarring sound beside him, that also attracted the notice of Captain Roche, who turned hastily about, eying his captive with a dull, suspicious glance. " What would you? Prithee take heed how thou trickest me. God's murrain! I look on all that folks are busy at with a hundred eyes. So run not thy head against a stone wall, or thou mayest find thyself worse than a boggling fool," he exclaimed with some incoherence.

The next moment, however, he rubbed his bleared eyes with mazy astonishment, as he beheld the well-knit form of the young Hospitaller drawn up erect, his arms free, and with his bare and glittering sword in his hand. After a moment of stupid wonderment, with a yell, as if he had beheld a wild beast couched to spring at him, the bravo started up from his settle, but was instantly struck down with a fierce blow of the young knight's gauntleted hand. He fell senseless on the ground, his face becoming quickly covered with blood, while, setting his foot firmly on the ruffian's breast, Richard

Plantagenet hesitated for an instant, whether or no to pierce it through with his tempered brand.

" What the foul fiend is this ?" shouted Tony Vulp, after a gaze of drunken wonderment. Then seizing his own weapon, he endeavoured to stride towards the scene of strife. But the young knight bided not his approach. Time was too precious for further tarriance. He therefore rushed upon the knave-errant, and grasping him firmly by his strong and bull-like neck, tripped up his heels, and hurled him to the floor in a minute's span. He then dashed the head of the half-drunken bravo on the hard oaken boards to stun him, and, wresting the poniard from his vengeful grasp, would inevitably have terminated his career, had he not been prevented by the more cautious hosteler.

" Nay, good sir knight, prithee slay him not. By the Blessed Virgin, that were needless blood-letting! Go hence with what speed thou canst. Thy horse is ready accoutred without, and perad-venture there is yet time for the safe accomplishment of thy purpose, which, mayhap, I guess, and the which God speed thee on !" he exclaimed, as he drew Plantagenet back.

" Wilt eat, for thou hast fasted o'er long already, I trow ?" added mine host eagerly.

But Richard Plantagenet declined, and thanking the honest hosteler heartily for his timely interference, he hastily quitted the building, and, finding his horse ready held without, vaulted into the high-peaked saddle. He proceeded in the direction pointed out by his late enforced host, and speedily entered Richmond Old Park by a narrow road that proved nothing better than a bridle-path.

During this untoward delay, the appearance of the night had much changed. The atmosphere had become dense and close, while the sky grew rapidly blacker and blacker, shading the moon and its beaming streams, till it assumed the dreary darkness of a winter's night. Very soon, and ere he had advanced many paces in his now headlong gallop, red, blue, and yellow streaks of lightning, vivid and hot, flashed

athwart the murky sky, illuminating it from the
eastern to the western horizon like unto a fiery
dome, while rain began to fall heavily and the
stunning peals of thunder reverberated around
with crashing roar.

But the Hospitaller neither heeded nor perceived these evidences of the quick impending
storm, as he forced the noble steed forward to
its utmost speed. On, on he sped with tight
held rein, nerveless seat, and unpitying spur.
On, on, good steed! On, on, holy knight! Not a
minute or a moment lose; for she whom you
love, whom you seek, is, alas, in a sore and
cruel plight!

CHAPTER IX.

Rescue or No Rescue.

STORM of no common potency was thus being heralded in, as the lone horseman pursued his headlong course. Between the pauses of Heaven's fierce artillery, there appeared to brood something akin to awe amid the solemn stillness of the skies, hushing even, as it were, the desolate grandeur of the streaming earth beneath. But on he swept, heedless of all; on along the grassy plain; on beneath ancient oaks whose broad gnarled limbs the storms of many centuries had vainly striven to uproot; on beneath gigantic beech trees with their silvery stems shooting loftily upward, sprightly sycamores, majestic elms festooned with the clinging ivy, and dark chestnuts; on, while the roar of the bandog and the hoot of the screech-owl, sounded weirdly on either hand; on, with spur and lash, through the picturesque, romantic park, where Fancy might have revelled rarely, calling up from the woody depths the Dryads of the forest, from out its flowing stream dainty Naiads, while Dianic nymphs showed themselves amid the rocks, Satyrs burst forth from the sylvan earth, and hideous Fauns, with their stiff pine wreaths roared lustily in the distance; on, on, still on; until at last the rein is drawn beneath a mighty oak, directly facing the ancient palace he had so impetuously set forth to reach. Under the dense shadow of its befriending branches, he dismounted, secured his matchless steed, and then strode forth to reconnoitre. Although combining an heroic soul with a noble form, luckily for himself, and still more fortunate for the safety and well-being of his betrothed, he did not rush headlong to the main entrance, and demand admittance, and the immediate restitution of Aveline More, as was his first intent and fiery purpose. Reason and caution, while re-

suming their sway, had shown him the mad folly
of forcing himself thus single-handed amid a
host of enemies.   He must achieve his purpose
by some subtle surprise, and with that object he
strode round the palace, performing a complete
circuit, while observing narrowly every form and
feature pertaining to it.   Then coming back
to the spot where he had left his horse, he
became convinced that he faced the state rooms
of the building, and most probably that portion
of them where his gentle Aveline was lodged.
He gazed eagerly and inquiringly at a large
casemented window on the first floor, through
which from within rays of artificial light threw
their lack-lustre on the thick wet herbage
without.   While thus intently watching, thus
anxiously awaiting some positive evidence in
favour of his hap-hazard conviction, a wild cry
of a sudden pierced the air, and a shrill womanly
scream echoed far near, which for a moment
rendered him fixed and pallid as stone, but the
next roused him to fierce and impetuous action.
He started forth from his leafy shelter, flew

across the intervening space, and reached the walls of the palace just beneath the illuminated window. Searching anxiously about for some means by which to ascend, he observed, with a gush of wild joy, that the mantled ivy, which we have stated covered a greater portion of the antique structure, was of great age, and that its thick limbs and gnarled branches offered an easy and secure mode of access to the chamber above for a young athlete or for a brave heart. Quick as thought, and amid the gleaming bursts of the fierce lightning and the roar of the red artillery of Heaven, he clambered up the natural ladder, and speedily accomplished the ascent. Reaching the window-sill, he looked in and beheld a scene which curdled his blood with the wildest indignation and filled his soul with the most fiery rage. There, in very sooth, was his beauteous Aveline, from whose face naught of its rare and angelic softness had been robbed, nor from whose form had fallen any of that inexpressible and virgin modesty for which it had ever been so famed. She still looked lovely—lovely beyond nature's fairest picturing, while piteously beseeching mercy and help, and while struggling violently in the arms of a richly-attired cavalier, whom the Knight of St. John at once recognised as his former opponent and determined rival, Sir John Perrot.

He tried to force the casement, but it yielded not to his most frantic efforts ; and at last, in the wildest fury, he dashed his gauntleted hand against it, splintering it and sending the crashing glass flying on all sides with a startling din.

"Thunder and wounds ! What is that?" exclaimed Perrot, with a wondering start, withdrawing his amorous embrace, and striding, with undignified haste, to the window.

He looked forth, and at once detected the fiery-beaming face of Richard Plantagenet.

"By my father's beard, 'tis the monk-knight!" he exclaimed. "Now shalt thou meet with thy deserts, sir springall;" and he threw wide the casement, and, clutching hold of the stout surcoat of the young Hospitaller, he shook him roughly, with the intent of dislodging him from his hazardous perch. But he either overrated his own strength, or under-valued that of his antagonist, who gave him an answering clutch, from which there was no retreating; and, while thus the hands of each were fiercely employed, neither could strike a blow.

"Thou dastard knight and recreant!" furiously shouted Richard Plantagenet. "Thou hast broken the laws of all nobility and chivalry, and, by the Holy Sepulchre, I'll have your heart's tainted blood if ever we meet in open lists or fair-fought field. Of a troth, thou art no longer fit company for honest folk."

"Insolent rapscallion! Let go thy murtherous clutch, or, 'fore George, I'll have thee scourged from hence to London!" exclaimed Sir John Perrot, as he felt himself being drawn more and more from his balance while leaning forth from the window.

"Leave thee go! Never, until I have rescued Mistress More, though in the attempt we should both pass into eternity. So come thou forth, sithence I cannot in to thee;" and then, using his utmost strength, and while utterly indifferent of the consequences to himself, the Knight of St. John jumped from his standing amid the stout old ivy, and through his weight, and by exerting his utmost strength, at length succeeded in dragging the burly and powerful form of his antagonist over the window ledge, and down they both fell, battling fiercely together, to the ground.

For a few fleeting seconds, Plantagenet conceived that his ribs were broken to pieces, and that he was dying; then the darkness of utter night appeared to descend on his eyes, and he imagined his soul was speeding from his body. That sensation, however, remained for a space of time scarcely calculable. Then came a rushing sound in his ears like the tramp of a legion of iron-hoofed steeds sweeping past; flashes of red fire started up before his eyes, as if the whole world was undergoing a mighty eruption; but these consequences of his fall in like manner quickly sped, and as his strength and energy returned he found he still clasped, with rigid taughtness, the thick bull-neck of his antagonist, who, in his descent, had struck his head against some protruding stems, and lay helpless and insensible, even as one dead.

Plantagenet started up, and hastily tying his opponent's nerveless limbs, and otherwise securing his person, he remounted to the window above, and, with anxious haste, jumped into the chamber. He found Aveline in an extremity of hope and fear, anxiety and dismay, kneeling and pouring forth many a fervent ejaculation to the Blessed Virgin. He flew to her side, he threw his arms around her, he drew her lovely form to his breast, and called aloud her name. With a radiance of joy, which lighted up her seraphic beauty as though beneath an unseen sunbeam, she started from him as if in doubt, then flew to his arms once more,—

> " Crimsoned with love, with terror mute,
> Dreading alike escape, pursuit—
> Till love, victorious o'er alarms,
> Hid fears and blushes in his arms."

But on a sudden he drew back, and looking into her pure, untainted face, he besought her to tell him if his rescue had come in time. " Oh, speak—speak, or let my bursting heart out with this cold steel !" he exclaimed, with wild intenseness.

" I am all thou would'st have me, my Plantagenet. Words cannot say more, and thou wilt believe in my assurance," she answered, while burying her blushing face on his guardian breast.

" As truly as in my own existence do I believe in it," he replied, in tones which vibrated through the enamoured soul of the beauteous girl. " But come, my beloved, let us away. We must not lose an instant, or our flight may yet be marred."

He wrapped around her his own large priestly cloak, drawing the hood well over her richly tressed head; then lifting her in his arms he approached the window, and attempted the descent. After a slight delay and some trouble, he accomplished this in safety. He then sought his good steed beneath the sheltering tree, and raising Aveline placed her on it, and then quickly vaulted up behind her. Feeling more assured when thus fairly ready for a flight, he rode up to where the bruised and discomforted Sir John Perrot lay in an utterly helpless, but now conscious state.

" By my father's beard, sir monk, thou shalt not long exult! And mark ye, I will not be accountable for the issue of our again foregathering in the lists at meridian on the day appointed!" exclaimed Perrot, with guttural fury.

" Thou hast my gage, and by it I spurn and defy thee. With lance and with brand, on horse or on foot, I will maintain against thee and all thy false line, that thou are no knight— no worthy noble—to have thus insulted a high-born lady. St. George be my warrant that I will keep my vow, thou traitherous bastard and unmanly coward."

These words to me ?—ha!" shouted Sir John, utterly exasperated, and vainly endeavouring to rise.

" Ay ! In very troth to thee, and none other, as, an I meet thee in the lists, I will most surely prove on thy body," retorted the Knight of St. John, drawing off his horse, and urging it forward along the pathway by which he had approached.

" 'Tis a pity thou hast not a cock's-comb in thine head-gear, thou no less monk than knight.   'Sdeath, it maddens me to see thee play Sir Launcelot after this fashion ; but, 'fore George, I will not suffer this indignity to pass unpunished in our wager of battle !   So look to it, I say—look to it," shouted Sir John Perrot ; but the other heeded not, even if he heard, the threatening words, as he speeded on his way through the leafy wilderness of the Park.

The storm had subsided almost as quickly as it had arisen, and, as they cantered leisurely onward, the bright monarch of the night skies burst forth anew, shining aloft like a globe of molten silver, and lighting up most radiantly the dewy grass, the rivulets which trickled along towards the banks, and the sleepy stream of the noble river ; as well, also, every leaf on the lofty trees, every violet cup and blade of grass on the grateful earth. Onward and without molestation sped the twain. Aveline was carefully grasped within the stout and guardian arms of her lover, who, ever and anon, looked down on her lovely face, as if on an angel's book, with the glowing light of a passion which might almost have instilled a returning warmth in the bosom of a statue, e'en moulded, like St. Cyprian's, in snow. His spirits rose on Hope's exulting wing, as they thus knittingly careered along on their return. He had rescued her, he had saved her, she was all his own; and a species of sorcery in his high-born soul appeared to tell him—a Pythia which seemed to prophecy—that he should be great, and both happy, even amid the dangers and pitfalls of that tempestuous age, and that an inheritance beyond the Prophet's dream, or the Enthusiast's hope, should still be theirs.

CHAPTER X.

The Tilt Yard at Whitehall.

THE morning of the grand tournament, to be
held in honour of the beauteous favourite
and newly proclaimed Queen, dawned, and the
sun burst forth with the cheering power of early
spring. The morning falconet from the Tower
heralded in the gladsome holiday, and well-
betimes was the whole city agog. Brightly the
sunlight spread over the rural suburbs of the
enwalled city, dancing upon the dimpled waters
of the pure-streamed river; while, already in
blossom, the lilac groves that bordered it were
filling the fresh air with their aromatic fragrance,
and while every flower and blade of grass around
were merrily glistening in the morning's world
of dews. It was, in fact, one of those delicious
spring morns wherein all nature appears to

rejoice, when the newly burst leaves are greenest and freshest, when the lively lark soars blithest from the verdant mead, and floats nighest heaven, when a myriad other plumed and feathered songsters warble forth their gladsome notes in hedge and copse, when the blessed sunshine, each fleeting moment, summons some fresh object into new life and renovated beauty, when all that greets the human vision is pleasant and bright, and when all that sounds upon the eager senses is in delightful harmony and melodious accord.

Forth from the narrow streets and close atmosphere of the ancient city, forth through its embattled gates, forth into the open unbricked district beyond, along the Strand, shaded by trees putting forth their greenest leaves, and bordered by the foxglove and blue-bell in ample luxuriance, came a long, continuous stream of rejoicing citizens. Some were astride pack-saddles, bearing behind them their buxom wives on cumbrous pillions, others afoot well supported by a goodly family attendance, while yet others, more well-to-do, bestrode steeds richly caparisoned, beside horse litters wherein reclined, in luxurious indolence, their superbly attired dames. All were arrayed in their holiday attire, much of which was of rare quality and colour, for that was an age delighting in rich garnitures. Forth, too, vieing with one another in prodigality of human decoration, velveted, jewelled, embroidered, and plumed, marched in serried ranks the divers guilds or campanies of the city, each preceded by its gonfalonier, with rarely embroidered banners bearing some peculiar device. And forth came numerous black and grey-robed monks, with the chiefs and principal officials of several monastic establishments, ambling along on sleek mules. And forth also, a few apart, some in small groups, and others marshalled in bodies, rushed the famed 'Prentices, youths composed for the most part of very inflammable materials, and prone to take fire on the slightest application of heat. They were young men of respectable lineage, who were bound to the best traders of the day, such as grocers, drapers, haberdashers, skinners, ironmongers, vintners, and other respectable artificers or tradesfolk. They were one and all armed with their unfailable large cudgel or club, the well known and formidable weapon of the London 'Prentices, and in the use of which, whether as a quarter-staff or missile of offence, they were remarkably expert. Even in the heat and height of a mêlèe, a skilful swordsman stood but little chance against their well-directed attack. And forth, too, amid the numerous and medley throng, came more than one bold and gaudily-bedizened courtezan, who—

> " From patches justly placed they borrowed graces,
> And with vermilion lacquered o'er their faces."

On came the miscellaneous crowd of rejoicing cits, along the Strand, than which, with its broad gardens, and lofty trees, its embattled turrets and famed mansions, nothing could be more picturesque; on past St. Clement's Danes Church, and the famed wells of St. Clement's;

past the Holy Well, and the " Old Roman Bath " still in existence ; past St. Mary's, and the great Maypole chronicled in these lines in the ' Dunciad '—

" Amidst the area wide they took their stand,
  Where the tall Maypole once o'erlooked the Strand ;"

past the Savoy Hospital, formerly the palace of Henry III ; past Exeter 'Change, with its booths or stall-like shops, and its much frequented menagerie ; past the several Inns of the lords spiritual and temporal, through the intervals between which might have been discerned the woods of the Long Acre, the vineyard and convent garden pertaining to the estate of the abbot of Westminster, the village of St. Giles, subsequently one of the most fashionable suburbs of London, the church of St. Martin's amid green fields and vivid hedgerows, and the Dogs'-fields, Leicester-fields, Windmill-fields, and the fields adjoining Soho. On, on they came to the hamlet of Charing, which, according to one author, consisted of no more than a dozen hovels; past the cross of devotional love, which fanaticism destroyed when it broke forth in the early part of the seventeenth century. On, on towards Holbein's Gate, beyond which lay in sombre magnificence the ecclesiastical structures of the great Abbey of Westminster—a very paradise of monachism.

The river, however, was the great highway of the period, and, indeed, the most convenient one for kings as well as subjects. At that time it was at the height of its glory, as the great silent thoroughfare of the metropolis, and on this occasion along its broad and gleaming surface floated many of the gilded galleys of the nobles and gentles, and more numerous still the sumptuous barges of the wealthy cit, whose elaborately-carved and gilded prows, variegated standards, and pictured keels, were richly relieved by the burnished glitter of the noble stream, within whose waters salmon and trout were daily captured in considerable numbers. In this noble stream the monkish legend records, that Edric, a fisherman of Westminster, who convoyed St. Peter to the consecrated site of the Abbey, drew up his miraculous draught of salmon.

The Tilt-yard at Whitehall, where the jousting was appointed to take place, was situated on the western side of the vast area facing the palace so lately designated York Place—the fallen Cardinal's sumptuous residence. It formed, it may be said, almost a part of the palace itself, so nigh and so closely allied were the buildings of the one to the out-buildings of the other. Henry VIII had erected the Tilt-yard on a grand scale, as an indispensable place of festal resort. He caused a space of two hundred and fifty yards in length by one hundred in width, to be enclosed and encircled by high walls, against the inner side of which were raised large scaffolds, consisting of a treble tier of seats, partioned from each other at certain intervals, like unto boxes in a theatre, for the accommodation of the general public ; while, at the southern extremity of the enclosure, a sumptuous gallery had been erected and set apart for himself, his queen, and court. This latter erection was richly decorated with crimson velvet, and hung with cloth of gold. Attached to the main enclosure were several smaller ones, devoted also to purposes of exercise and recreation, such as a tennis court, a bowling alley, a *manége*, and last, though certes not least in the mind of the bluff king, a cock-pit.

The entrance to the tilt-yard was through a superb, double-turreted edifice, commonly known as Holbein's Gate, which also formed the chief approach to York Place, or the palace of Whitehall as it was to be ever thereafter designated. A large palace hath been fairly likened to a city in miniature, and of a surety might the one-time magnificent structure of Whitehall come within the category. On the east it extended along the river's front, with considerable depth, to Scotland Yard ; while on the west it reached as far as the open space in front of Westminster Hall. Though irregular in the extreme, and with, as we gather, little pretension to plan in its arrangements, yet the palace of Whitehall

was eminently picturesque and imposing, from
its vast extent and antique conformation.   In
the gardens, which were on an equally extensive
and sumptuous scale, the velvet moss and the
tufted grass were shaded by many a druid oak.

Facing the royal gallery, and just in front of
Holbein's Gate, around which were assembled
a numerous cohort of archers, pikemen, arquebusiers, lancers, and men-at-arms, to keep order
and prevent rioting, were the barriers, attended
to by a number of pursuivants ; while just within
these, in a long and animated line, were the
chameleon-hued and silken pavilions of the
various knights about to engage in the different
courses of the gallant tournay.   Over the entrance of each tent was hung the device and
motto of its occupant, while in front stood a
herald in his gorgeous tabard and plumed cap.
Beneath the audience galleries were ranged a
numerous array of peddies or horse-boys, hold-
ing the champed bridles and burnished bits of
barbed horses, caparisoned in massive trappings
of steel and brocade, all restive and eager for

the martial fray. Apart, and in one corner of the tilt-yard, was a tent of considerably larger dimensions than the pavilions of the knights, which was kept for the use of the seriously hurt or wounded in the divers tilting matches of the day, and which was presided over by a sage, a leech, or a chirurgeon, as he was variously designated, who wore the robe and hood which had been peculiar to his craft for two centuries previously, and the imposing appearance whereof exerted more than half the sway the disciples of Galen held in those days over human credulity. They were not very learned, as may be surmised; but what lack in skill in the mediciner's art they one and all possessed was made up, much after the fashion of the present day, by pomposity, verbosity, quackery or impudence.

Within a pavilion of pale green silk, situated about midway in the long line, and just ere high noon, were seated Sir John Perrot and his never-failing companion, Sir Ralph Sadler, who, on this occasion, acted as the other's esquire.

" How goeth the time, Sadler ?"

" I have no horologe with me, but what sayeth
the sun on the dial-plate above Holbein's gate ?"

" Scarce meridian yet, an I see aright, and I
am as athirst as the parched sand.   By the
mass, give me to drink, friend Ralph, of yonder
measure of barley ptisan and usquebaugh
mixed; 'tis more cooling than wine, albeit less
palatable."   And he drank plenteously of the
soothing posset.   " Gad's life, 'tis not o'er much
amiss when one's blood is afire; and now give
'me my bottle of daffodil water, 'twill in turn
cool my face's skin."

" The rough handling of the Hospitaller thou
still feelest, Perrot.   He not only hath courage,
I trow, but, it would beseem, a touch of iron in
his sinews."

" Pest, it is nothing, save a scratch or two
not worth the leeching.   Though for all that,
credit me, I wish the young lion eternal God
speed to the devil," exclaimed Sir John Perrot
impatiently, while lolling somewhat painfully on
his hard settle.

" 'Twere better, in my thinking, to send thy love-junketings thither," said Sadler with a smile.

" St. Venus, nay! The beauteous Aveline will ever shine like a sun amid lesser stars, and foul fall me if ever I relinquish my pursuit of her," said Perrot in a resolute tone.

" *Pasque Dieu!* I have known, ere this, that love can turn many a bearded man into a puling boy. But, certes, I deemed not to behold your highness so deeply smitten. Thou hast, of a verity, a broad bosom for the reception of amorous impressions; and methought that thou couldst at all seasons find ample room for two attachments at once."

" By all the saints, and there are enow for a rattling oath, I care not for other fancies! I tell thee, Sadler, I love, I adore this lily flower, and all the more that she resembles not the gaudy beauties of the court, but twins it well with the Hebe of the gods; and, by the mass, I will pour out my heart's best blood ere she 'scapes me ! I will yet luxuriate in her arms of animated snow, or seek the icy ones of death."

" I cry you mercy, Perrot; but thou forgettest, in thus pursuing this fair Circe, that she answers not thy amorous leanings.   Hast marked these lines :—

> " Fain would'st thou love, and all thy soul
>   Yield to the burning god's control."

But alas! Perrot mine, another couplet answers well thy case—

> " Oh ! vainly all things, Love, with thee conspire;
>   Her soul reflects, but warms not in thy fire."

" Go to, Sadler,—go to!   I arede not thy pleasantries.   I was warned by her who nursed my infancy against all lay-women, whom, in her pantheistical fervour, she termed syrens and instruments of Satan.   Let that pass, sithence I've long since outgrown her wordy trammels, and by St. Peter and St. Paul to boot, am self-capable of handling my own wayward-ness, wheresoever it speedeth.   But hark to thy ear.   Methinks I can trust thee, Sadler."

" 'Sdeath, yes, with anything save a goblet of wine !" answered Sadler with a light laugh.

"Or a pretty maid; eh, my Sadler! Nay, man, pucker not thy brow so demurely, unless, peradventure, thou intentioneth to eschew the world and become a noisy professor of religion, like some of the craft, never missing a mass or a daily office, wearing an enormous rosary, crossing yourself a hundred times daily, smearing thy goodly person with ashes on Ash-Wednesday, and stuffing thy stomach with hot cross-buns on Good Friday, and viewing, evermore, thy father confessor as the sole keeper of the avenue heavenwards. By all the oaths that ever were sworn, thou would'st make a rare monk!" said Sir John Perrot, with a jeering laugh.

"Thou canst not, by thy flouting words, take the flavour from mine advisings," answered Sadler. "I'll warrant me, womankind will prove the rock upon which thy goodly bark will ere long be wrecked. Didst not Pembroke yestreen well assert, that thou shouldst not trust friendship or faith in woman, for 'twas like biding the devil in the skin of a snake. He further said there was poison and treachery in all they uttered or performed ; in their nods and leers, their curtsies and caperings, their counter-smiles and dumb-show, and that when they weep with one eye they can wink with the other."

" Holy martyrs !—was ever the like of this vilipended afore ? Gramercy, Sadler, what art thou coming to ? Methought but now thou hadst a leaning for monkish demureness ; but, gad's my life, thy words show a hankering after anchorite celibacy ! But a truce to this flummery in thy speech, only suited to a pilgrim overburthened with years and crimes. But hark ye, and trouble me no more with thy advisings to the contrary ; Aveline More shall be mine, if, by my father's beard, I have to make her so in the world's full blazon ; and, for her unmatched beauty, I will uphold it to the stretch of doom."

" Thou must needs first bestow the Knight of St. John, who hath a face and form to win favour, in some safe keeping, or of a surety thou wilt not complish thy will therein," opposed Sir Ralph Sadler, in visible astonishment at the other's announced determination.

"I have but now to run joust with him, and I stake my manhood 'gainst his that in the issue of our duello I destroy his pretences, flimsy as they have ever been. But why tarries the youthful fire-eater? They do say lover's feet are not asses," said Perrot, forgetting his own earliness.

"He will be here betimes, despite all hindrance to the contrary, as thou mightst witness from the events that have already ta'en place," said Sadler, with a sly smile.

"Ay, ay! God's fury, and his malison to boot, be on those bungling villains, who, though twain to one, did not stay him in his speed. But tell me, Sadler, dost not mark some strange significance in the lady's eyes? Methought she was void of all blissful vision," exclaimed Sir John Perrot, as he drew forth an exquisitely chased silver pouncet-box filled with fragrant essences, and applied it to his nose.

"Master Verstegans hath her in tender treat-

ment ; and it minds me that Dame Rumour hath
it he can complish for a certain season all he
aspires to. But wilt not arm, my doughty
knight? See, some intelligencer hath arrived
announcing the advent of the court. Shall I
summon thy armourer ?"

" Ay, do so, an it please thee, friend Ralph.
Ho, there! Bring hither, varlet, my pyne
doublet, and then don me yon suit of Milan
steel!" shouted Sir John, immediately subjecting
himself to the skilful hands of his attendant,
who in a trice harnessed his broad muscular
person in complete panoply.

"I crave service, Sadler; prithee truss my
points more firmly. I owe thee thanks. Now,
good friend, hand me some of the contents of
that long-necked flask," and he emptied, at a
draught, a horn of brandy.

Meanwhile, in a large wooden hut, or fixed
pavilion, erected hard by, for the use of stranger
knights, or those who from rank or position
could not indulge in the prominence and show
of their more privileged co-mates, and apart

from the rest of the company using it, stood Captain Roche, with Tony Vulp for an esquire on this martial occasion. They were both leaning against the side of the erection, looking out through a small square opening upon the tilt-yard and the varied preparations going on therein.

"A truce to such a play of words, Vulp; a baby's hand, I trow, may strike discord from a ghittern's strings, so I pray thee cease, thy words are all frothy!" exclaimed Captain Roche.

"Go to—go to, I say! Have I not sworn a secret oath—an oath which to break wert per-dition—that wherever I meet this soldier-monk within all this good realm, on plain or hill, in city, camp, or field, there, by Lucifer, will I do him to death, though the next moment be my last!" answered Tony Vulp, in a revengeful and vehement undertone.

"Art aweary, then, of thy own life? For, 'fore George, ere you spit him like a lark, this Knight of St. John will give thee some worse blood-letting! But, Tony, I oft do marvel how so great a blusterer as thou became so matchless a villain," said Roche, with a grim smile of disdain.

"Thou art a toad of the devil's spawning to vilipend me so; and prithee bethink thee, worthy captain, that thou art in all ways as deep in mud as I in mire, however villainous the soil may have proved," retorted Vulp, looking sullenly fierce.

"Mayhap you are turning more chicken-hearted than afore, and canst not rest o' nights because of thy pricking conscience," continued Roche, with another sneer, while playing ominously with his rapier.

"'Sdeath! I must needs confess I cannot at all times sleep to my liking; while visions of evil omen, like warning spectres, haunt me more often when I do," answered Tony Vulp, in a tremulous tone of voice.

"Then I avise thee, Tony, to lie awake to thy doom, in which there would be reason also, as thou wouldst then have further time for plotting evil like unto thy betters. Or, perchance, 'twere best for thee to go to some jolly round-faced member of the Black Friars—Dan Launcelot, for instance—who will assoil thee, and ease thy overweighted conscience of its grievous burthen of many a ruthless deed," added Captain Roche, jeeringly. "But as to this Knight of St. John, I owe him methinks a turn of my own free will, which I trust to pay him ere many suns go down."

"Then, gadslife, lose not the opportunity which this day's *mêlée* will offer! He is, I trow, completely enmeshed, and must needs run his courses within these lists; and if, perchance, his grace, whom you wot of, handles him bloodlessly—then, 'sdeath, in the general onslaught ordered by his Majesty, we can of a subtlety speed him quick and surely to the devil!" eagerly suggested Tony Vulp.

"What! Doth the pummelling he bestowed on thy head-piece the other eve excite such vengeful ire in thy soul, that thou must needs have his lifeless carcass to welter in the midnight dew, or broil in the noonday sun?" said Roche, mockingly.

" Foul fall thee and me too, if, for all thy gibes and sneers, my quarry scapeth me long! I will track him as a hunter tracks his game; through rain and storm, the moonlit mist and midnight gloom, if need be, o'ere he flies my vengeance. If a turn offers after he hath enforced his gage of combat, 'sdeath, let him look to it that my dagger finds not a way to his heart!" said Tony Vulp, while pressing his scarred forehead, which still ached, nathedoubt, from the pounding it had received on the floor of the hostelry at Mortlake.

" Gramercy! Have thy way, if thou canst reach it; but waste not further words, nor wear the day in such child's play as this; for certes we have other business on hand than splitting the fine hairs of your bloody casuistry," said Captain Roche. " But, by the mass! yonder comes the Knight of St. John, and attended, too, by some haught youngster. See, Vulp, he beareth himself as loftily as the most proud-plumed helm in Christendom."

And so it was. Amid the numerous knights

flocking in through the well-kept barriers, Richard Plantagenet, attended by an esquire and page, and bestriding a coal-black steed, with flowing mane and tail, and of wondrous spirit and power, entered upon the gay and martial scene. Being unfurnished with tent or pavilion, and not caring to share with strangers the one erected for common use, he turned his steed aside, and took up a position somewhat apart, and under the shadow of one of the side galleries. He was harnessed in a complete panoply of black mail, even his barred helmet being surmounted by three lofty raven plumes, while over all was thrown the dark hooded-cloak of his proud and warlike order. Horsed and accoutred thus sably, his erect, well-knit form seemed to tower pre-eminently above his compeers; and, as he entered and moved to his solitary position, he became for the moment the cynosure of all eyes.

Having drawn rein, his slim and plainly attired page approached, observing in an under tone—"Bethink thee, sir knight, of all that has been urged on thee for thy safe-keeping in the coming tournay. Though I have secured thee the leader of the city 'Prentices for thine esquire, 'twere better not needlessly to raise the cry of " Clubs," unless thou art first foully set upon or become endangered through some damnable emprise."

The Knight of St. John smiled with a slight curl of his handsome lip and a dilatation of the nostrils, as if in contempt of the danger against which he was warned.

" Of what foregathering mischance would you caution me, Mistress Barton," he demanded with haughty indifference.

" Nay, I know not of precision, but too well, I trow, that death ever spreads his snares in secret, and thy outspoken honesty hath reared thee enemies even on the throne. To bestow thy candour into safer keeping than this world offers wert no ill-deed, I trow, for the rulers of these cloudy days," answered the page with warm earnestness.

" If any violence be offered to womankind, it

is both in my knightservice and manhood to battle him to death who dares to offer it. For that cause am I here, as well as to redeem my gage, which the court minion, Sir John Perrot, hath taken up on behalf of his false and upstart master," exclaimed the chivalrous Hospitaller, with his usual recklessness.

" Oh, peace to your valour, dear knight, I pray thee! These are times in which the human tongue must not trip too glibly."

" Now, out on thee, Mistress Barton. First take better heed of thy own dangerous pratings, ere thou chidest mine. Prithee, too, remember I sanctioned not thy earnest entreaty to attend me at this mortal arbitrement to gain thy schooling, but solely, of a troth, to give thee better opportunity to witness the gaiety of the quest, and the prowess of the tilt-yard, as thou thyself didst urge upon me."

The Maid of Kent smiled slightly, while her eyes beamed with a wondrous subtle fire, as she looked up and answered the young warrior monk—" Think so still if so it please you. My soul, however, accuses me of other urgings, and more forcibly than is pleasant, or for my peace."

Fraught with the nectar of the impetuous passion which pervaded her whole voluptuous nature, a greater warmth instilled itself into her words than she had purposed showing. Her heart's fever was one of those enthralling, though sudden fancies,—

> " That comes like the lightning,
>   All withering or brightening."

The Hospitaller gazed down upon his disguised page in some considerable amaze ; and in perfect ignorance of the occasion, demanded in a more gentle tone—" Of what rave you, and what, by St. George, means that deepening and ever deepening blush ?"

" As to my raving, holy knight, heed it not. Let it pass through your memory as a murky cloud of night upon some traveller's path. But accept my deepening colour as the pledge of my regret for words idly spoken, and the gage of my esteem for thy knightly soul," she answered in some dismay, and with considerable perturbation.

"So be it! I'll accept the latter, Mistress Barton, as a good periapt against thy former prognostications of coming ill."

"Yonder advanceth the King's Majesty and the Queen's Grace!" somewhat excitedly exclaimed the esquirely disguised 'Prentice, as he stepped forward.

The next moment there was a grand, but to modern and more tuneful ears, nathedoubt, a very discordant flourish, or fanfare, of trumpets, announcing the approach of the royal train, which immediately filed its way, in becoming state, through a privy entrance into the Tilt-yard, and up into the elaborately fitted gallery prepared for its reception. Henry, richly bedecked and be-jewelled, after being duly heralded in all set form and state, strode to the front, leading his newly proclaimed, though not so lately wedded wife, whose smile was all radiant with joyous triumph, whose lip quivered with proud and elate emotion, and who had never before appeared at once so born alike for love and command—a *Venus celestis* arrayed in and surrounded by the pomp of earth. With the vivid bloom of her complexion, the warm perfume breathing around her, the gaiety and triumph which sparkled in her eyes, the pliant grace of her movements, the subduing softness of her voice—she seemed to embody every attribute of the invisible goddess. She was arrayed in a boddice of silver tissue, which confined to admiration her perfect shape, with every heave of which sparkled jewels of great value and number, while a diadem flashed on her fair brow with gemmed excrescences as if it were a coronal of brilliant stars.

Close beside her was a beauteous bevy of the fairest maidens, whose lustre and pearliness were alone outshone by their transcendent queen, and again surrounding these was a goodly phalanx of nobles and gentles glittering, some in armour, others in jewelled mantles of flaunting colours, prelates in sacerdotal pomp, but among whom the purple mantle of the fallen cardinal was conspicuous by its absence, together with numerous pages, domestics, and yeomen in the most gorgeous liveries.

Taking up their station beneath the royal gallery, were a crowd of yeomanry of the guard in their scarlet gaberdines, with long poniards and partisans, arquebusiers with their uncouth and heavy matchlocks in hand, and halberdiers with their long stout pike-headed staves held stiffly aloft.

But little of all this gorgeous state and glitter did Richard Plantagenet notice. The glistening galaxy of beauty and wealth in the royal gallery, the gilded vases filled with rare exotic flowers, the numerous banderols, the braying of trumpets, the festal glories all around, the rude splendour of suits of armour, bird-beaked helmets, flaunting feathers, and trapped bridles; the moving and shouting masses of the rejoicing populace; the glitter, the wit, the laughter, the noise, all floated indistinctly and unobservedly through the suddenly spell-bound vision and distraught soul of the Knight of St. John.

He was gazing upon the group of lovely damoiselles that surrounded the Queen, and while doing so, his blood seemed to throng so thickly about his heart that for a while he could scarcely breathe. His face, clearly seen beneath the uplifted visor of his aventayle, in the garish blaze of noontide, was paler than the ashes of a pinewood fire when the dawn shines on it, while many a pang shot athwart his palpitating heart as he perplexedly and dismayedly recognized, amid the other attendant beauties, the ever-loved, ever-discernible features of Aveline More. But his heart-throbbings somewhat quieted down, when he perceived a noble-faced courtier advance to and whisper her, in whose features he at once distinguished those of her father, Sir Thomas More.

" 'Tis strange, though, how she came hither, for her presence at court hath ever been against the leaning of her loving sire," remarked the

Knight of St. John, more in reverie than in the anticipation of being overheard.

" 'Tis Sir John Perrot's doing, be assured," answered the Maid of Kent, who had perceived the sudden and unaccountable excitement of her companion, and watched with many a querent glance the direction in which his eyes were so rigidly fixed, while recognizing, almost simultaneously, though with an unpleasant feeling at her heart, the mysterious presence of Mistress More. " But well, I wot, may you start, dear knight; for of a surety the plot thickens, and an additional wheel within the many already encircling may now be discerned."

" What further mischance would you hint at?" enquired the Hospitaller with visible uneasiness.

" See you not the cowled form standing behind Mistress More, and whose lynx eyes pierce this way, as if already he penetrated my well-chosen disguise. Ay, look too, Sir Knight, he whispers his blissful penitent, and points thitherward, and she, as if all-visually gifted, in answer to his hint, fixes her lustrous orbs on us.　He, too, glares upon us with vulture eagerness," exclaimed the Maid of Kent, with a strange foreboding sickening her soul.

Richard Plantagenet gazed eagerly amid the courtly throng, and soon perceived the pale, sardonic features of Dan Theodulph, who met his glance with a smile of dull malice and hatred plainly discernible.　The excitement of the young knight, however, was more than passive; the inward commotion of his fiery spirit acted on his muscles, and as the high-mettled charger he bestrode with so knightly a grace felt the nerveless goad, he plunged forward and reared snortingly upward.　This action drew all eyes upon him, and numerous were the mixed remarks, patronizing and hostile, made upon his noticeable appearance.　But meanwhile there was something demoniacal and wild in his own fixed gaze.

"Good knight and loyal, I pray thee patience. Back thy steed again.　'Twill be thy certain ruin if thou doest aught rashly now.　Bethink thee of thy gage, which thou art here to second and uphold. I pray thee to withdraw from further notice," most earnestly implored Elizabeth Barton ; and not without avail, for the young warrior-monk backed his steed into the shadow again, for he felt the gage had been thrown to a fate which he must meet, whate'er the clouds might portend which threatened thus unexpectedly around.

" You mark the sub-prior's habit?" asked the Maid.

" Yea, yea. But why blears he so murtherously on you ?"

" Know you not a manslayer's shoes are always red, and of a surety leave footprints which sooner or later set the blood-hound of justice on his track ? He knows the full range of my ken, which detects the burning plague-spot in his heart, that hath already sunk him deep in hell's hot flood, and fears lest I should break my leash and hunt him down," said Elizabeth Barton, with a sultry gleam of her wild dark eyes.

" If 'twere so,—methinks wert safer in his

dastard monkhood to keep thee in goodly fellowship with him," said the Knight of St. John.

" Nay, not so with him. He is, I well weet, of that rare school of deceit and villainy which, when it hath wrought all it aspires to, turns off the instrument with abhorrence and fear," answered Barton, with panting earnestness.

" What fearful toad of the devil's spawning must this beetle-browed monk be ?" said Plantagenet, in a dreamy tone.

" He is one who, howe'er he mislikes me, hates thee worse than poison, death, and hell," said his companion, with strange significance.

" And with what cause, prithee, Mistress Barton ?"

" Cause, forsooth !" As for that, the cause is yonder," said she, pointing towards Aveline More.

" Ay ! By St. George ! Is it so ? Let him look to it. An I catch him in flagrant delict, that moment will certes be his last, though from her vestal eyes methinks dark vice must needs turn away," impetuously shouted Plantagenet. "But now to meet this court minion, this feather-bed soldier, to swell whose peacock pride this attendance is drawn together. I perceive the marshals are clearing the barriers and preparing for the courses."

"Beware of the hellicate rake, dear knight. Thou standest on peril's brink;—take heed! Use discretion, for 'tis wisely asserted to be the better part of valour, and then thou mayest be able to penetrate what at present it beseemeth are well-nigh impenetrable mysteries," urged the Maid of Kent, running over all her mental perplexities with the light and varying fancy of womankind.

"On my faith, and as I live, the lance that I shall break with this disguised scion of a usurping royalty shalt not end the strife 'twixt him and me! There is but one stream which shall stay us, and that rolls out of the Black Valley. I arede not how it chances that all his deeds of arms are outblazoned by his deeds of guile. In the coming onset both shall be levelled, and amid the world's approving eyes, if portents and prophecies have not hovered over my head in vain."

Thus speaking, he set spurs to his steed, and bounded into the knightly arena, where the rest of the various champions were being marshalled, previous to passing beneath the royal gallery in procession. He had no fear of the issue, no momentary hesitation of his own prowess. Ere he could have known doubt or dismay in the martial lists or in the tented field, all mankind must first have turned recreant. Oft has it been averred, and with heaven-descended truth, that there is but one real nobility, and for which no human proof is needful; for Nature, the most unteinted lawgiver, signs its charter. Of a troth was this most marvellously so in the face, in the soul, and appearance of Richard Plantagenet, and well attested was its public recognition by the approving looks and the murmurs of applause which greeted his entry into the lists. So thought, but more amorously, the Maid of Kent, as she intently watched his

movements, and prayed earnestly for his success and safety: praying, mayhap, much after
the same fashion as Dugdale hath worded it
of a knight of even more antient times—

"O, holy St. George! O very champion!
    O undefyled and most holy knight!
   O gemme of chivalry! O very emerand stone!
    O loadstar of loyalty! O diamond most gwyght!
    O saphir of sadness! O ruby of most light!
  O very carbuncle! O thou mantese of Yude!
  Graunte him thy helpe—thy comfort for to fynde!*

* Dugdale's Baronage

CHAPTER XI.

The Deliverance of Arms.—Bearding the Lion.

DESCRIPTIONS of tournaments have employed so many illustrious pens and filled so many admirably written pages, that it needs not I should weary my reader's patience by setting forth anew the minutiæ of the gallant pastime. Indeed, so much has been indited on the subject that the illustrations have become as trite as they are picturesque, as familiar as they are interesting. We shall, therefore, omit the record of many a feat of prowess in the divers tilting matches which ensued, as well as all the exercises of agility shown in riding at the quintin, practising with arbalettes, pitching quoits, slinging the bar, and such like, contenting ourselves with mentioning those incidents which relate more immediately to our chronicle.

In the same spirit we shall pass over in silence the usual dazzling details of the galaxy of female loveliness, of the eyes of beauty glistening like the silent stars, and of the elegance and coquetry which inspired, added grace to, and honoured the various passages of this grand assault of arms.

Leading the knightly calvacade, rode Sir John Perrot, sheathed in a magnificent suit of armour, and mounted on a beautiful roan steed, which was armed with a spiked frontlet of polished steel, and had a plume of feathers dancing on its proud head, a jointed *crinière* to defend the mane, and an embossed poitronal or breastplate to protect its stalwart chest. He made a gallant show, and loudly was he greeted by the discerning and approving multitude of spectators. But more loudly cheered by the men, and more admiringly scanned by woman's sparkling eye, was the tall, erect form of the Hospitaller, encased in its sable panoply, bestriding a coal-black steed, whose fine limbs, compact and nervous carcass, glossy skin,

flowing mane and tail, swelling nostrils and
rolling eyes bespoke its pureness of breed
and highness of spirit. The young knight
bore himself haughtily ; for he had ere then
signalized himself in those chivalrous exploits
which alone, in that more martial age, rendered
men glorious in the eyes of their fellows.
Numerous and varied were the company of
knights who followed the chief warriors of the
day, and gallant and martial appeared the
cavalcade as it wended its way round the lists
and beneath the royal gallery, where the numerous and brilliant suite of high-born dames and
maidens of honour, of chamberlains, equerries,
squires, and pages made a gallant show beside
the brilliant queen. Some wore the long two-
handed sword ; others the formidable battle-
axe, diamond-pointed at the extremity, called
the *maillet*, the handle terminating in a three-
cornered point, termed a tusk—the rondelle, a
round plate of iron, being affixed to guard the
wrist ; while others there were who had slung
beside them the estoc and death-dealing mace

a club with a large circular end spiked all round. All bore their lances aloft, with the silken bandrols gaily flaunting in the air; while each was accompanied by his esquire, more or less richly attired, or variously armed.

As Sir John Perrot caracoled beneath the royal gallery, the King took off one of his buff gloves, richly embroidered and perfumed, and flung it to his quondam son, exclaiming the while, in his usual guttural voice and bluff manner, " Thou art, son of mine, thy king's as well as thy father's champion this day; do thou nobly thy devoir, and let this be the insignia of thy worth and our approval."

"I will hold it, your highness, against all comers, so help me God at the day of doom!" answered Sir John Perrot, fixing the glove in his waistbelt.

" Thy boast shall meet its reward, false knight, an thou be one! That trophy shall be wrested from thee, or my life's-blood be outpoured on these lists!" shouted the Knight of St. Jóhn, with a grim look of defiance at both his opponent and his royal backer.

Though great the astonishment which spread throughout the courtly throng, yet there was not a little unspoken admiration expressed in the faces of many at the daring of the young knight. Aveline More caught the sound of his well-known voice, and her beauty lit up with an expression of sparkling joy and welcome, its roseate hues on a sudden all deepening; while her beauteous eyes were aglow with the depth of the emotions swaying her heart. She leant eagerly forward, and appeared, by the instinctive fixity of her gaze, as if she really looked on light once more, and beheld the ennobled manhood of her lover; while the love-flames of her heart shone from her eyes like holy light from sacred shrines. Sir John Perrot saw her at once, and recognized, with a smile of, certainly not unmixed, triumph, her agitation and eagerness. He, however, with considerable fervour, exclaimed, " Prithee, Mistress More, bestow one favour upon your most devout and humble admirer—you who mayest, even amid this galaxy of beauty, be uninvidiously proclaimed love's oracle."

But the lovely girl answered not, and shrank timidly back into her former less observed position, while a hectic colouring of some secret solicitude flushed over her face. Henry, meanwhile, with a frowning brow and flaming eyes, retorted upon Richard Plantagenet, "Methinks, Sir Launcelot, thou art too much afire in thy speech to be of any great note in tilting, albeit thou hast oak in thy backbone. Look to it, however—'slife, look to it, I say ; for, an thou art beaten in the coming jousting, I will take the issue as a judgment on thy guilt, and punish accordingly thy outspoken treason, which we do not misremember ! Who, think you, will gainsay my judgment ?—ha ! But come—dally no longer : marshals, clear the courses. Sound the charge ! Let the jousting begin, and this haught springal to a recreant's doom."

" I am no recreant, Sir King, as I will prove against thy body in the lists an thou darest face knighthood and honesty conjoined ; or if thou art amort to do so, then look to it ; for I will not belie my untainted lineage, but will of a surety blazon thy usurping royalty and unkingly knavery abroad in every court. This will I maintain with my sword in the heart of whoso denies it—be he king or beggar," shouted Richard Plantagenet, in a haughty tone and with flashing eyes.

Every one expected some sudden outburst of wrath from the unbridled and passionate king. But they were mistaken, or disappointed, as the case might be. Henry, for one long uncertain moment, glared with the most revengeful fury upon the young knight who thus ventured to beard him amid the noble assemblage that surrounded him. The next, however, he smothered, albeit with an evident effort, the mad rage which was so ready to burst forth, then beckoned Sir John Perrot to approach him, and whispered him hoarsely for a fleeting minute, after which he waved his hand for the commencement of the martial sports.

Largesse was first showered amid the crowd who had forced the barriers to witness the presentation of the various champions to the king; and, after the scrambling that thereupon ensued had subsided, the warning waftures of the marshals' wands of office drove the populace back to the public limits without the barriers.

The athletic sports were the opening ones of the day, and in them neither Sir John Perrot nor Richard Plantagenet took part. After these had been gone through with divers degrees of success, the tilting was commenced by a young knight, mounted on a fiery Spanish barb, who acquitted himself with grace and skill, and against whom Sir John Perrot first poised his lance, and was proclaimed the victor. Then, after a while, the heralds sounded anew their trumpets for another course; and barely had their flourishing ceased when both the Knight of St. John and his burly opponent burst forth from their resting-places, and simultaneously took up positions at opposite

ends of the lists, with their spears feutered, or
set in rest. Though Sir John Perrot out-
matched his opponent in his stalwart form and
burly carriage, yet there was something more
of the experienced tournayer in the young
knight's appearance. The latter's powerful and
supple limbs were so perfectly sheathed in his
well-tempered suit of mail, that their shape was
admirably developed, while the strong muscles
and vigorous sinews stood plainly out, as if
only covered by silk. He was all strength,
sinew, and activity, and amply fed with the
' day-god's living fire.'

"Let do!—let do!" was in a trice stento-
riously shouted by the heralds, and forth, like
an arrow from the bow, shot each determined
jouster. The onset was furious, too much so
indeed for any decisive issue. They met in so
fierce a shock, that Perrot shivered his spear on
the breast of his young antagonist, while that
of Plantagenet's pierced his opponent's shield
and rent his surcoat in pieces, while each regained the opposite side of the course swift and

unshaken as a whirlwind. Reining up quickly, they each turned their mettlesome steeds, and, on receiving fresh lances from their squires, prepared to renew the knightly contest.

" Hast picked me a sturdy lance this bout ?" eagerly asked the Hospitaller.

" Ay, of a troth ; and one that, beshrew me, will not give as did the last !" significantly answered his squire, the disguised 'Prentice.

" Ho, false noble ! Defend thy life, for it is in danger. By the bones of my royal fathers, this shall be no combat à *plaisance;* so look that thou aimest unerringly, or I shall of a surety dash thee from thy steed, and do thee to death amid this dank soil," shouted Plan-tagenet, all athirst for action and excitement, while possessed with a furious determination to achieve the victory.

" St. George and our Lady be my speed ! I am at thee ! I cry you mercy—come on !" retorted Sir John Perrot, with equal eagerness.

They rushed again, lance in rest, furiously at one another, the courtly throng looking on with bated breath, for their purpose was evidently deadly. In a moment they met, and the next Sir John Perrot was rolling upon the sand of the lists, his courser galloping wildly and unmastered around them. The Hospitaller was also badly shaken, being well-nigh bent back to his saddle by the force of the concussion, and beneath his heavy *destrere*, but, quickly recovering, he galloped back to his end of the lists, and giving up his steed to his esquire, he dismounted, and hastened to the centre of the arena, where Sir John Perrot had already started to his feet, little the worse for the rude shock of his fall, but madly enraged at the galling mischance. The passions of each combatant were fiercely aroused, and when they both their willing weapons bare, without let or hindrance from Henry, who presided as judge of the field, and whose decisions or decrees, as such, were ever absolute, they as well as the spectators knew the combat had resolved itself into one *à l'outrance*. In Plantagenet's mind, however, that had been a settled determination from the beginning.

The guards and blows were fiercely given and quickly made, and for several spell-bound minutes did the almost equal contest continue, without any grave advantage to either side. But the Knight of St. John had not merely practised in a school of arms or in the tilt-yard; he had seen active service and gained his knighthood on more than one stricken field in foreign wars. Determined to triumph, and at once end the pretensions of his opponent, he, after acting on the defensive, and for a while wielding his keen blade with wondrous skill, as much with the object of exhausting his adversary, as for the purpose of concentrating his own powers, suddenly uplifted his heavy two-handed sword, and with a swoop, and in the blind fury and determination of heated passions, he brought the gleaming blade down upon the helmet of his adversary with a crash that re-sounded loudly throughout the tilt-yard. The feeble and hasty guard stayed not the crushing blow, nor did the well-tempered steel of the polished helmet; and in another second Sir

John Perrot lay as one dead, stunned and profusely bleeding on the sands.

Sir Ralph Sadler with divers pages and
attendants hurried forward, and, after Plantagenet had snatched the king's favour from his
belt, bore the senseless noble to his pavilion,
where, his armour being unbelted, he was quickly
attended by the mediciner, who, with the aid of
simples and healing salves, soon restored him
to his former well-being, albeit he remained
somewhat bruised and dizzy, and withal sadly
crestfallen.   Meanwhile, the Knight of St. John
having been vehemently cheered by the populace, and grimly regarded by the courtly circle,
remounted his held steed, and clutching with
wild eagerness a lance, set forward at an easy
gallop towards the royal gallery, close beneath
which he suddenly drew bridle.   He then lifted
himself in the stirrups, and, outstretching his
lance, struck it roughly against Henry's broad
breast; after which he withdrew again at an
easy pace to his former position.   All were
amazed at the boldness of the act, and Henry

himself not the least so. For the touching of shield or person was, in chivalry, one of the acknowledged modes of offering a challenge. Henry watched the retiring form of his young antagonist, with the fierce sullen glance, and the eyes of flame, of a bayed lion. There was, even in his best of moods, something of bloody terror in the aspect of this tyrant and licentiate. and, at that moment, there arose a wrathful moodiness in his look that might have scared a less determined spirit than that of Richard Plantagenet. When the latter, however, had regained his post and observed the direction and peculiarity of the king's glance, he returned it with one even more haughty and defiant—one in which the spirit of his kingly forefathers plainly spoke.

"Ho, sirs, why stare ye all amort!" shouted the king at last in his habitual manner, that affrighted more than any open outburst of the fierce rage churning within. " It shall be seen how Majesty can punish school-boy insolence, sithence there are not found those of his subjects who can. We will ourselves join in the *mêlée*, having come panoplied for the purpose. We will lead the side of blood and loyalty, and yonder upstart, sithence he ventures to brave peril so wantonly, that of plebeian mould. See it so arranged, my lords of Suffolk and Norfolk. I will leave ye twain to marshal my array and get the gear in readiness. What will you wager on my behalf, my lady marchioness,—my queen that is, and shall be," he added, turning to Anne Boleyn, as the two dukes departed in compliance with the royal bidding.

Fruit, confections, and wines were distributed throughout the royal gallery ; while, in the pause which thereupon ensued amid the official list of the day's sports, the hungry and thirsty populace set to work, after so high an ensample, to more frugally appease their stomach cravings,— no doubt much in accordance with the same fashion, though mayhap somewhat more primitively, and certes less luxuriously, than the frequenters of race-courses and other popular sports in modern times indulge in.

The preparations for the grand assault of arms between two equally divided forces, called the *mêlée*, or medley, which imitated the confusion and hurly-burly of a battle, were soon completed, and the opposing miniature armies thereupon drawn up in battle-array at opposite ends of the lists. Then Henry, having previously betaken himself to his tiring chamber beneath the gallery, issued forth, and mounted a superb milk-white steed, with wide-flowing mane and tail, and of the freest and most powerful pace. Its colour was set off by its crimson chanfrein, its nodding crest of crimson plumes, its broad poitronal with crimson tassels, and its saddle with rarely embroidered crimson housings. Henry was magnificently accoutred, and appeared, by a strange coincidence, or some fanciful conjuncture, completely panoplied in white. His very armour, overlaid with plates of silver, shone white in the glittering sunlight; while his surcoat, but for the crimson embroidered device and motto of the Marchioness of Pembroke, wrought in the centre, was also of the same snowy colour. In fact, his whole arms, costume, and horse-trappings, were of rare magnificence, and shone resplendent in the eyes of the admiring and shouting populace.   He was immediately styled the White Knight, while Richard Plantagenet was, with equal reason, designated the Black one. The twain, by their conspicuous garniture, were the most noticeable amid the array of combatants, which numbered a dozen on either side, all handsomely attired, with their plumes, or *lambrequins*, waving in the breeze.

Silence being proclaimed, a herald went through the usual formula of setting forth in stentorian tones the several conditions of the contest. These we need not repeat ; for are they not written again and again in divers other chronicles ? The squires stood within the barriers on either hand to assist their masters in the event of discomfiture or mishap. Amid those who were drawn up on the side of the Knight of St. John was the thick-set figure of Captain Roche, though so completely embedded in his heavy mail as to be—as he nathedoubt desired—perfectly unrecognizable. Behind him stood his quondam squire, Tony Vulp, who, beneath a russet doublet, wore a slight hauberk of iron wire, and had his rapier beside him, while he impatiently unsheathed and sheathed his long dagger, in some dark rumination, as he eyed maliciously the erect form and noble bearing of the Knight of St. John. "By the devil's teeth, but this is glorious. 'Twill go hard if I cannot in the confusion about to ensue give blow for blow, and, 'sdeath, wipe out the marking of my blood in his!" he muttered, in a hissing tone, between his teeth.

A clear space of about a hundred feet intervened between the opposing squadrons, in order that sufficient impetus might be given to the shock of the pending encounter. The spectacle just previous to the onset was one, we may easily conceive, of no slight splendour and interest. The opposing lines of combatants, each eager for the fray, and each leaning forward in excitement for the preconcerted signal, with lances well poised, their fiery steeds snorting and pawing the soft soil, while tossing aloft their foamy heads, amid all the chivalrous panoply of crests, helmets, surcoats, emblazonry, glitter, and plumes, one restless, moving mass of colour, brightness, and gorgeousness.

Suddenly, amid the silent hush, the voices of the heralds proclaimed aloud, " Let do ! let do !" The next minute, the clash of arms, the splintering of lances, the clouds of sand tossed upward, and hither and thither, by the straining hoofs of the mettlesome steeds, the chattering fanfare of the opposing trumpets, the cries of squires and pursuivants, the falls of riders and horses, and the deafening uproar of the surging and excited populace, announced at once the commencement and the height of this grand passage of arms. Each knight was allowed three lances, so when having splintered one he immediately procured another, and again rushed forward to aid the side for which he contended. The contest lasted not long ; for in the space of ten minutes, or little more, it was perceived that the side of the king had triumphed; for there remained opposed to Henry and five of his flushed and successful followers only Richard Plantagenet and his very doubtful supporter Captain Roche; the rest of the combatants on either side having been thrown from their saddles, and scattered in utter derout.

"Yield thee, Sir Black Knight! Thou canst not say we win unfairly, nor we, St. George forfend, that thou hast contended ignobly!" exclaimed the king, in a jovial voice; for his anger had all vanished beneath the gladsome gleaming of success.

"Yield to thee! I, a Plantagenet, yield to any son of man! Nay, Sir White Knight; I will, by your leave, only yield as a wave that flows away until it is high enough to overwhelm. I and my steed are once more afresh; so, have at thee, and let the issue be proven on this single course," shouted the Knight of St. John, in a loud voice, and with flashing eyes.

The events of the next few minutes are almost indescribable, so quickly did one with

lightning flash succeed the other.   The king in
reply had but time to utter, " Then God assoil
thee, thou untamed cub," ere Plantagenet was
upon him, and so sudden was the assault, so
startled the king, that ere his steed could be
urged much beyond a walk, or himself offer
opposition, he was hurled with unprincely
haste from his hitherto well-kept seat, while
the Hospitaller swept swiftly and tauntingly
past. The latter turned as quickly as he could,
and met midway two of the king's supporters ;
one he with equal success and impetuosity
unseated, while the lance of the other splintered
against his well-tempered breastplate.   But in
this final onset his own and last lance was gone ;
but, determined not to yield, he drew his sword,
the flat side of which he was, according to the
laws of tournay, at liberty to use, and once more
plunged forward against the remaining foes,
while loud and continued applause cheered him
on.   But he was here overpowered, for the lance
of each of his remaining opponents struck him ;
one sent his helmet flying from his head, while

two others, by main strength, bore him from his saddle to the ground. But, though unhorsed, he still remained unconquered, and, rising with his sword closely clutched in his powerful grasp, he stood at bay, determined to lose his life sooner than yield. The king having recovered his overthrow, and bethinking the young knight so overcome that he might claim the honour of placing him *hors de combat*, stepped lightly and eagerly forward, sword in hand, exclaiming, "Yield thee, now, sir knight, I will suffer no further arbitrement. So, prithee, own thyself, after this thy last hard tussle, well vanquished."

"Never, by the Holy Sepulchre!" cried Plantagenet, and was about to rush forward against the king, when of a sudden, being struck down foully and treacherously from behind, he fell stunned and bleeding at the very feet of Henry.

"'Fore George, he is a matchless youth—a most valiant Cid!" exclaimed the king, after his surprise at this unforeseen termination had somewhat abated.

But his nobles and followers crowded round him, and he could not longer behold what happed to his luckless foe, who, though still and powerless as the dead, was roughly set upon by more than one of the king's guards, and among them Tony Vulp, who shouted out, and with an eager voice, " Let me to him. By God and the fiend, I'll care for his safe keeping! You do not laugh, good people, and yet what is more diverting than to see a rogue caught in his own springes." And he pushed his way within the circle formed round the fallen champion, and knelt down beside him. But ere, with his heart of stone, he could carry out his dastard and felon purpose, the page and squire of the insensate knight came breathlessly up amid the foremost of an eager rushing crowd, who had forced the barriers at the termination of the fray.

" Ha! coward, dastard!—what would you do?" eagerly exclaimed the page, as she caught one of Vulp's arms, which was compressing in a very muscular manner the throat of the insensate knight, while he was uttering a strange volley of blasphemous curses, mingled with pious ejaculations.

"Slave to be spat upon in the market place. Let go thy murtherous fangs," shouted the squire, dealing the ruffian a blow with his club, which sent him reeling back stunned and bleeding. The squire then added, as he endeavoured to clear a space, "How now my masters! What mean ye crowding in thus, limiting the air needful for my noble patron's restoring?"

It would seem at this moment as if the Hospitaller enjoyed a degree of twilight consciousness, for he made a weak and fruitless effort to rise. Suddenly one came from the king with orders to secure his person, asserting he had been guilty of treason and lese majesty. But the disguised 'Prentice whispered to one or two young men of the citizen class respectably attired, while they again muttered quickly to others amid the throng, and shortly the signal for a brawl with the cry of "Clubs, clubs!" was echoed far and near. The next moment a rush took place towards the centre of the arena, and

as Plantagenet was borne forth by his disguised
squire and two others of the company, he faintly
perceived the gleaming of swords as they were
raised to strike at him and his bearers.   But at
this moment—the very hair-line verge between
life and death—a body of the invincible 'Prentices rushed eagerly in, and by their numbers,
strength, and determination speedily swept
away, as with a flood, all hostile opposition to
the further rescue of the Knight of St. John.
Many of these gallant 'Prentices wore pyne
doublets, which were calculated to resist the
points and edges of the best-tempered weapons;
and, with the prowess they one and all displayed in the use of their formidable " clubs,"
they fought their better armed opponents with
comparative impunity.   Great indignation was
expressed by these wild youths against Tony
Vulp, and, as he recovered and slunk like a
whipped cur away, he was censured, jeered at,
and flouted on all hands.

While Richard Plantagenet, having lapsed
again into insensibility, became alike indifferent

to the indignities intended for him by the satellites of the despot, and to the careful tendance and numerous accompaniment of his allies, he was conducted to Whitehall Stairs, and thence by water to the Monastery of Blackfriars.

Sir John Perrot, though still dizzy and ill at ease, hurriedly threw aside his armour, and, having assumed a manteau, or robe of scarlet, rarely embroidered and trimmed with ermine, the attire usually worn by knights on state occasions, proceeded, with the aid of Sir Ralph Sadler, to the royal gallery, to pay his court, and pour out his fulsome homage into the pure ears of the excited, anxious Aveline More, who, looking like the white moon-flower, was already beginning to fear that a dark cloud was uprising in love's summery heaven.

CHAPTER XII.

Baynard's Castle.—A Wolf in Sheep's Clothing.

DURING the long hours of the night succeeding Richard Plantagenet remained
in a state bordering betwixt stupor, fever, and
convalescence. On his arrival at the wharf-
stairs, in front of the 'Three Bells,' within
the sanctuary of Blackfriars, he was, by the
directions of Elizabeth Barton, at once borne
to Baynard's Castle, which—though, as we have
shown, standing just without the precincts of
the great monastery—was in all ways considered
to be within the bounds, and subject to the
several immunities and peculiar obligations
pertaining to the sanctuary-town of the Black
Friars. His bearers thereupon crossed the
small wharf in front of the conventual hospice,
and, passing through a swing-gate, entered

the main yard of the famed castle, and thence
proceeded direct to the presence chamber of
Raimond Verstegans, who, having dismissed
the bearers, and all other tendance save that of
the Maid of Kent, bled the insensate knight,
washed his many bruises with rare medicaments
—how compounded we cannot analyse—and
forthwith ordered him to a sleeping chamber,
where perfect quiet was to be enforced.

The divers proceedings thus going on around
him, Richard Plantagenet beheld as in a dream,
dismally and unclearly.   Some faint recollection
he afterwards had of his first swooning and
subsequent rescue, then of the river and its
gay and glittering movement, of his carriage
through some of the intricacies of the antique and
massive castle, and of the healing and soothing
restoratives applied by the great astrologer. He
then, as it beseemed, lapsed into a heavy slumber, nigh akin to insensibility, through which,
however, he possessed a vague consciousness
that he was carefully nursed and tended by a
female form, which flitted to and fro without

noise or warning. When at last, just as the first streaks of dawn were diffusing themselves amid the failing beams of the fast sinking moon, he was rousing himself to a clearer perception of his state and its surroundings, he of a sudden felt a pair of warm velvetty lips fervently pressed upon his clammy brow, accompanied by a moaning, distraught sigh. This appeared to act as a spell, rousing him in a moment from his swoony lethargy; and, on his opening his eyes, and turning his head around, he distinguished the retreating form of the Maid of Kent passing away, like unto one of Spain's dark-glancing houries, behind the arras covering the doorway of his chamber.

On his more complete resuscitation, the Knight of St. John glanced enquiringly around his apartment, and perceived that the casement of a window between two lofty pillars, emblazoned with a rich Gothic painting, was open, allowing the cool fresh air of early morn to be wafted up from the river below. He beheld, too, that in the ample tiled-fireplace a pan of sack-posset was set upon a chafing dish to warm, while beside him, upon a low settle, was an old peg-tankard, containing ptisan—a fever drink, made of barley, boiled with raisins, liquorice, and other ingredients. Thus having taken gauge of the outward world, his mind immediately reverted to the varied and exciting scenes with which his wayward life had been so lately commingled, and mazy and chaotic in the extreme were the voluminous thoughts which thereupon intruded. The image of Aveline More—his soul's first idol and its last—was, as may well be supposed, the supreme disturber in that mental conflict; and well hath Shakespeare uttered it—

" But oh ! what damned minutes tells he o'er
  Who dotes yet doubts, suspects yet strongly loves !"

But when, after a few minutes of painful vaguery, he at last dwelt on her vestal eyes, her honest love and simple faith, her untutored innocence and guileless imagination, her fairy

witchery, and the peerless enchantment surrounding her—Hope, the celestial encourager
of youth, involuntarily mingled sunshine with
his dismal reveries.

In the midst of his moody thoughts, the
sounds of softly approaching footsteps made
him look up, and, with a start, he at once
recognised, in the cowled and hooded form
which had thus silently and mysteriously intruded upon him, the stalwart figure and sinister
features of Dan Theodulph. Ere he could
express the amaze he felt, and in his looks
exhibited, the sub-prior exclaimed, in his usual
calm, smooth-spoken manner—

" Our reverendissime hath bidden me hither,
ere matins is tolled forth, to make inquiry concerning thy health, sir knight, and thither,
therefore, have I speeded. It beseems thy
wholeness is not much affected."

" Commend me in all affection and dutiful
obedience to the lord prior, and tell him I am
little the worse for the foul treachery shown
me yestermorn, and that, by our Lady's aidance,

I shall hope to visit him on the morrow," answered Plantagenet, shortly and stiffly.

" I will convey thy messagery betimes," said Dan Theodulph; and then, glancing furtively round, he approached close beside the pallet whereon the sick man lay, and in a low, though somewhat husky voice, added, " Dost know what manner of nurse-tendance thou hast had the night through ?"

" What needs it that I should enquire, seeing I am in all things beholden for the aid and care shown me," answered the Hospitaller, evasively.

" 'Twas one, I trow, who taketh what con-cerneth thee somewhat more to heart," said the sub-prior, with a significant glance.

" I cannot guess the colour of thy meaning, though I may the personage to whom thou referrest," said the Hospitaller, with calm austerity.

" Methinks, sir knight, to one gifted as thou art in the lessons of the world beyant the cloister, it needs no years of study, no learned lore to read love's language. I weet well that the voice of Nature, speaking in the gentle air, and breathing in the odours of the wild flowers, is not more easily recognized than Love's expressive tokens on face and heart. Its light is like the sun's. The heart discerns its beams as does the night-thralled earth, day's banner of radiance! Oh, its presence is not to be mistaken. And canst thou surely have looked upon it and discerned it not, or, regarding it, have dismissed it from thy breast and brain, as some winged vision of thy night-bed?"

"By St. George, dan monk! I divine not thy meaning, though thou pratest so warmly of this same love, as an it were thyself who had known its power and felt its sting," answered Plantagenet meaningly.

The sub-prior gave one quick, unfathomable glance at the speaker, but displayed no other sign of understanding the meaning of his words. He was of far too subtle a nature to be betrayed into any exposure of feelings which he wished and was prepared to conceal. He had

long ere that adopted the Jesuitical teaching so
well described in a couplet by the bard of
Avon :—

" We'll mock the time with fairest show,
   Fair face must hide what the false heart does know."

So, as if wholly insensible to the point and
drift of the other's remark, he with very ready
ease answered—" Why !—how now ? Can it be
possible that in the warm and persistent attention of your present nurse and one-time page,
thou discernest not a feeling more glowing than
the sun at noon-tide, more amorous than the
moon at midnight. Certes, Mistress Barton
hath not, methinks, ever aforetime showered
her favours in vain; for, as report hath it, like
Phryne, the Athenian courtezan, she hath had
but to display her beauty to ensure success,
while moreover she can command in her soul
such delights as the genii of the sun alone can
summon by some all-potent spell."

" Mean you, dan monk, that Mistress Barton
feels aught illawfully towards me, or I aught

unknightly for her!" exclaimed Plantagenet, with haught impatience, whilst starting up on one arm.

"Nay, I said not so, sir knight; contrariwise, I meant but in a friendly spirit to avise thee of a success thou deemest not of. Bethink thee how enviable a matter it is, thus to have won without trial such a trophy as her heart, which, nathedoubt, might do honour to a monarch's throne," said Dan Theodulph calmly, albeit with one of his terrible sneers.

The Knight of St. John answered not, save by an impatient movement, and with a laugh of scornful incredulity.

"Thou laughest because thou canst not fathom the priceless value of that treasure, thine, all unknown to thee. If, peradventure, thou couldst, thou wouldst discern nought equal to it in this world of woful travail; nor neglect and despise it in the vain pursuit of a phantom which flies thee ever as thou pursuest, and which the Church hath already decreed can never be thine," said the prior, with solemn distinctness, and with a meaning it was not difficult to divine.

"Ha!—say you so, dan monk? Then list to what I have to say, and 'twere in reason to mark well my words," exclaimed Plantagenet, with angry impatience. "That same dame Rumour, of whom but now thou reportest some lying malevolence, hath more blackly whispered, that, in thy stolen and secret teachings to Mistress More, there hath ever been more of earthly passion than churchmanly lore, or confessor-like enjoining. Now, prithee, hearken what I, of my poor will, ordain respecting that blissful lady. Never more venture thou to approach her, on any business or under any pretext, for fear of a worse penalty than my ill-will. It bethinks me, in such a case, thou wouldst not be the first of thine order who hath been scourged for even a less offence."

"Scourged—scourged, say you? Ha!—" began Dan Theodulph, in a wild frenzied outburst, and with eyes that gleamed fiercely beneath his cowl. But with an effort as mighty as that with which the scorched, splitting earth sucks in the nourishing rain, he suddenly quenched the uncloistral storm that was on so nigh a point of bursting forth; though how fierce the effort at control proved, within his turbid and sulphuric heart, cannot be pourtrayed. With a mock calmness, which had something unnatural in its grating, he, however, continued, " Be not amazed, sir knight, to hear anger speak in me—a monk. I am human, though a cloistral devotee, and can no more bear such leprous aspersions than thou of a less reverential and of a more worldly brotherhood. I have been for many months past the authorized confessor and ghostly adviser of Mistress More, who is the purest and most virtuous of maidens, wanting nothing but the holiness of death to befit her for the white-robed company of virgin celestials, and whose voice methinks warbles forth the melodies of heaven, what time she sings, in the tone and after the manner of the angel Israfil."*

* The Angel of Music.

" Thou art right, by the mass, in so deeming Mistress More; and it minds me well that, without such Eve-like attributes, I hold womanly beauty to be a lure of Satan, a very poison in a jewelled casket; nay more, foulness and rottenness swathed in golden lace," said the Knight of St. John, significantly. " But, prithee, tell me, dan monk, how came it thou happed to be in attendance with the lady's chance appearance yesterday at the Tilt-yard."

" Attendance—chance—say you !" exclaimed Dan Theodulph, waveringly, while a dark flush momentarily mantled his features. " Know you not, sir knight, that the heads of all the religious houses within call were specially summoned to attend the king there, and that, my lord, our reverend prior, being indisposed, I thereupon went thither as the unworthy representative of our august monastery, and thereon perceiving—albeit much to my chagrin and fatherly fear for her—Mistress More, I did thereupon but give her such support and guardianship as such a presence and company needed. And never, knight, have I rejoiced more than on beholding, during thy fortuitous tarriance in their midst, thy victorious crest."

There was nothing fulsome in the latter sentence of laudation, for there was nothing of falsity in the truth it spoke. The sub-prior, as we have shown,—we trust with sufficient clearness,—seldom resorting to the Spartan gymnasium of self-conquest, naturally desired to behold all rivalry to his disloyal passions abased to the utmost and swept for ever away. He entertained almost more fearful and dismal dread of Sir John Perrot's untameable regard and determined pursuit, than of the more sure and welcome attentions of the young knight of St. John; and therefore, in the words he had last given utterance to, more of secret truth spoke than was habitual with one of his impenetrable and tortuous policy.

" In our Lady's name, wherefore ?" demanded Plantagenet, surprisedly.

" Because it is at ·all times well that the insolent should be abased, albeit in the midst of their power and pride. Doth not thy opponent in yesterday's quest cherish nefarious designs against a purity vowed, as thou must be assured, to our Lord Jesu, and the which, too, hath he not more than once sought violently and outrageously to carry into evil effect—and ere this would, nathedoubt, have succeeded in, hadst not thou, like a good knight and true, baffled his felon purposes, and saved the chosen bride of Heaven from such hideous profanation."

" Withouten doubt, monk, I have saved Mistress More, but for so doing I seek not your or the Church's commendation ! I hope for a reward of a very different complexion,—a reward beyant all human tongue-service," answered Plantagenet, coldly, and as if weary of the discussion.

" And one which, nathedoubt, you will obtain, when, on the completion of her vows, Mistress More remembers thy unmeasured services in her future prayerful outpourings," said the subprior, with a furtive glance, and with unabated purpose, while in the same spirit thereunto adding, " But, of a surety, art thou not already garnering the harvest, that thy good and noble deeds have sown and fostered, in the resplendent heart of the Maid of Kent. Nay, start not with the impatience of doubt. 'Tis proven, certes, beyond all dispute. Her glowing affection, though all untold as it beseems, hath natheless proved the observable cynosure that inspired that occult and mystic devotion to thy well-being, which your heart must confess to, even in its own despite. And let me, though lowly and humble I be, hold thee mindful of the gratitude thou owest for so spontaneous and disinterested a passion, and of what dishonour there would be in disavowing the flame thou hast, however unwittingly, fanned and fostered, and in so doing leave her naught but the wildest lamentings henceforth until she reach the gates of eternal Light."

" Go to !—go to, Master Dan Theodulph ! I need not thy doubtful schooling of my duties. Bethink thee, 'tis not in this instance Pedantry gulling Folly," retorted the warrior-monk impatiently; and then added, with becoming modesty, "But of thy self-imagined romance respecting Mistress Barton I credit not a word, nor would, were it even amid the most terrific sketch of Fancy. Bethink you, monk, that Love is a passion which broods in a lone breast. Nay, by St. George!—that is it not. Credit me, it is gendered solely in twain bosoms, which throb alike in weal or woe, and that rise or sink in unison. It is not meted out in Custom's falsest scale. To love, beshrew me, we must needs be beloved. I grant ye, an idol, divine or mortal, may be adored in reverence, albeit without return; but, by the mass, that engrossing perception of the soul worthy the name of love exists not betwixt humanity, until heart combines with heart, and both become linked by a bifold chain of genuine sympathy, which unites them ever after, even through all time, and the utmost bounds of space!"

At this moment, and ere the sub-prior could urge any reply, the Maid of Kent entered the chamber, and, without noticing the visitor's presence, approached the invalided knight. There was a strange pallor on her face, and a gloom as though some warm flood of sentiment, in which her soul had erewhile felt as if afloat, had of a sudden congealed : as though a freezing blast had blown upon the surface of some sunny lake, and iced it in the very heat of summer-time.

" There is one without who desireth speech with thee, if so be, sir knight, thou art at leisure and alone," she said, in a low and dizzy voice.

" Then I will hence, brother of St. John. *Benedicite!*" said the sub-prior ; and shading his face more fully with his hood, he departed, muttering to himself as he did so, " That Jezebel hath, medoubts not, overheard our converse. Perdition seize her ! She ever playeth the espial on me, her footsteps falling as soundless as snow on water." And the glare of an immortal hell shot forth from his eyes.

He had scarce left the chamber ere Cromwell entered.

CHAPTER XIII.

The Maid's Confession.

"SO, so, sir knight, thou hast learnt thou canst not play with flame and yield up the game, when thou listeth, unscorched. But a truce to jesting; for I am glad, and God be praised for it, that thou hast not yielded up the ghost before thou wast by moderate computation due in death's ledger!" exclaimed Cromwell, as he advanced and greeted the young knight, with a warmth and interest even to himself undefinable.

"I am thankful for your goodwill, Master Cromwell, and am glad thou art come to while away the time of impatient sickness. Thou, perchance, canst explain to me some of the mysteries in yesterday's doings, sithence I know

little that occurred after those false and dis-
honoured knights had hurled me from my
horse with a conjoint treachery," said Plantagenet.

" Marry, thou hast to thank thy womanly-
framed page that all of life left after the concussion was not squeezed out of thee by some
ruffian hireling, who seemed bent on wringing
thy neck, as oft afore, nathedoubt, he hath
treated fowls."

" Ay, so it was told me. But shines the
sun on a blacker miscreant than that knight
who treats with such rapscallions to do his disloyal and knavish will!" shouted the Knight of
St. John, in fiery indignation.

" If it be as thou deemest, he were surely
the very shame of knighthood. But at whom
points your suspicion?" asked Cromwell, with
eager interest.

" Canst thou, who perceivest so well how the
world wags, and how fortune ever drives, not
unriddle so transparent an enigma?"

" In the name of the master of mischief,

whom would you designate? Heaven forefend that you mean not Master Perrot!" said Cromwell.

"Whom else, think you, unless there be some significance in his incognito? Bethink you Sir John Perrot could not so attune his bloodthirsty thoughts, and that, too, with the usual anodynes that statesmen and rulers lay to their consciences, and ever gloss o'er their ill-deeds?" replied Plantagenet, with a scoff.

"Why, god-a-mercy, 'twere barely in reason, albeit he may be designated a shoe-tie of royalty, a very skip-jack of the court, and as such is not over careful of his honour or his acts! But I am minded that I have infinite reasons for believing thou hast a more fearful enemy nigher to thee, inasmuch as he is one who worketh in the dark, darkly; while Perrot acteth ever openly, though mayhap not choicely overmuch. I discerned the beetle-browed sub-prior of yonder friary as I entered, though he hooded himself closely. I oft do wonder if the tales abroad concerning him are of the truth, and how it may be possible so dark a spirit can give utterance to sentences so radiantly coloured and shining in devotional light, as he so oft doth."

" Aye, Master Cromwell, well mayest thou marvel; for if all be true of which Dame Rumour speaketh, he carrieth the sun-stroke passion of Romeo in his breast combined with the refined fiendishness of Iago, whilst outwardly he demeaneth himself as a mirror of Parnassus and a Hercules in theology."

" A true disciple of Plato, and of whom God forbodes that the Maid of Kent knoweth more I well weet than she dare mention in her prayers," added Cromwell, with a short laugh. " But ever when I meet him doth he stand as stiff as a saint in marble, and as one who seeks not men's herding. I fear he is of the class of smooth-spoken, lamenting hyenas, who hide their vices within the shades of the cloister, and whose resorts therein I am resolved to hunt out and wholly cleanse."

" Mayhap, Master Cromwell, he remembereth

the old saying, that a saint and a sinner both come to the same thing—a statue cut in flesh. But canst tell me some of the court gossipry, and more precisely the causes of Mistress More's presence in the royal gallery during the tournay?" asked Plantagenet, with visible uneasiness.

"Ha!—good sir knight, thither turn all thy mental fancies and heart yearnings, be the hour one of joy or sorrow," said Cromwell, with a quiet smile. "By my faith! See now how he blushes, for all the world as if he were a maiden caught kissing by her mother. But think you I pry into such Machiavelian manœuvres as court secrets and court deeds?"

"Ay, that dost thou, Master Cromwell, unless it be that, like your late master, you have spun the great web of your policy out of its manifold passions, follies, and interests, all for naught," said Plantagenet, impatiently.

"My master say you! Alack!—alack! Ill news travel fast, and there is that current this morn which saith that he who was all men's

master in this realm will own no man master
many more diurnals. Of a troth, his have
proven the most difficult and dangerous webs
ever spun by the subtle genius of one mortal
brain. They are, too, of such a quality that I
dare not imitate them, albeit my courage fails
not, nor does my faith waver. He who rolls a
stone down the mountain side cannot stay it
where he will. But mayhap it is my contempt
for human judgment that leads me right the
wrong way. But, pooh, pooh! This is not the
sort of moralizing for a sick man's chamber.
What saith Master More ?—' Enjoy life while it
lasts, and take death when it comes.' I have
much to say to thee, albeit not now, of that
good, rare man, whose example many might
imitate. I will speak to thee anent it when
time serves better. Thou didst ask of me but
now information which methought thine own
conceivings might have satisfied thee on. Who
canst thou suppose but his grace the king's son,
self-styled Perrot, did cause his royal sire to
summon Mistress More to court ; and though

sorely against her father's will and opposings, the summons was of such urgency, he dared not have adventured to slight it. She went therefore under her father's escort; and you know, may-hap, that his Majesty, being of notoriety a Solomon in such light matters as female beauty and female inclinings; and, not misliking the gentle lady's appearance, hath ordered her to court again on future festival occasions."

"Then she hath returned meanwhile to Blackfriars?" said Plantagenet, by way of enquiry, and with a sigh of wondrous relief.

"Of a troth, yes; where she may, I trow, abide more safely now, sithence her royal and amorous lover will perceive he can have speech of her without further rough handling. But hast heard the news which hath set all London agape?" asked Cromwell.

"Nay, how were it possible, seeing I am fettered thus to the bed-ingle by preconcerted treachery!" exclaimed the Knight of St. John.

"It hath so chanced that these men of the cowl and cassock have a glimpse of my plans, and are teaching each other the power of resistance. Lo ye, too, the whole body of St. Benedict is bestirring itself, and is railing loud and furiously against the promoters, abettors, and supporters of the New Learning. And certes, in this craft and misdoing of the monks, I am dexterously assayed to suffer, though they cannot scathe what the lightning hath spared; but knowing that I am a favourer and furtherer of Will Tyndale and his rare translations of the Holy Scriptures, they have at the instigation, as some assert, of Sir Thomas More, but more certes through the instrumentality of Bishop Tunstall, collected numerous copies of that edition, and have ordered them to be publicly burnt by the common hangman."

"That is not the way to unmaze the truth. Such acts will of a surety prove but further scarifying of an already dangerous wound," commented Plantagenet in a rapt tone ; for the leanings of his monastic education amid the chivalrous brotherhood of St. John had not been deeply ingrained with the fierce antique prejudices, and the blood-thirsty zeal aglow amid the general monkhood.

"It may well be that Heaven is aweary of the system of which these monks and their daily acts are the true unwholesome spawn," returned Cromwell, with vehemence. "Their abominations have been exposed to the light of noonday, and the king, whose avaricious grasp I persistently incite to lay hold of their hoarded treasures, begins to discover, beneath the snowy garment of would-be ascetism, the leprous blackness of Satan."

"I cannot go with thee, Master Cromwell, in thy wholesale vilifyings and purgings, so prithee, let us have peace on a subject-matter which may, perchance, breed ill-will, that, somehow, I care not to feel against thee," said the Hospitaller, with simple earnestness.

"Thou art, good youth, of sterling mettle, and art worthy to fill a higher and nobler destiny than that of lurking within a sanctuary. I might say of thee, in monkish Latin, thou art *factus ad unguem*,"* said Cromwell, eyeing his companion with warm interest. " And, forasmuch as thou canst not forswear all humanity, I am here, like the ancient schoolmaster, Dionysius of Syracuse, to rebuke thy noble pride, which wars more against thy own advancement than to the damagement of those thou esteemest thine enemies, and in all beseechance to urge thee to quit this land for a while, till the furnace of wrath, raging against thee in certain circles, be quenched. In other lands thy chivalrous manhood will meet many and rare occasions for its development ; and there no short-lived hopes, which, like wintry suns, possess but a small arc to blaze in the jealous firmament of the day, will longer rack thy generous soul. It is written that he who toucheth pitch shall be defiled therewith, therefore seek not to mingle the noble stream of your untutored nature amid the foul, effete sources of courtly vice, habits and contentions."

* Fashioned to a nicety.

" Is the voice of human sympathy silenced
for ever—will the strings of that universal harp
vibrate no longer. And will none be found
among the descendants of that glorious phalanx
who survived the disaster of Bosworth Field to
help me to my own again," said Plantagenet
lowly, and with a sigh.

" Such questioning shows me how little you
know the rate at which a man's honesty goes at
court now-a-days, or how all men begin to run
after self as the Alpha and Omega of existence.
His present Majesty is too stolidly seated on
England's throne to be worsted therefrom by the
spirit of the greatest warrior Christendom ever
beheld," said Cromwell, sententiously.

" Though loath, I am, natheless, apt to believe
thou art right, Master Cromwell, and that 'tis my
unripe acquaintance with the world which makes
me marvel at men's forgetfulness or baseness.
And this is no new thought, for long since have
I crushed the high hopes which one time bloomed
in the dark desert of my life ; and well may I
now perceive that so far as this land is con-

cerned, all is useless, cheerless, barren, and still as death. I will, therefore, away, to another land, to other duties, to other hopes, and let it be, kind Heaven, other rewards. I will but stay long enow to secure that treasure which lieth in this England, and which is so truly my very existence, and without which the pains of life were not compassable for a day."

Decision was one of the marked peculiarities of Richard Plantagenet's character, and, knowing this, Cromwell experienced a wonderful feeling of relief, perfectly unaccountable, at the other's suddenly outspoken resolution.

" I will not pretend to misunderstand thy words. 'Tis a prize worth the having, for brilliants are not always the gems we mate with in this life. All I have further to say unto thee, is not to lose the golden opportunity of saf passport to France, which I can at. the present time insure thee, by any long tarrying. Get thee well and strong as speedily as may be, secure thy treasure, and then hence without further tarriance, and God speed thee evermore."

"Yea, yea! I will away, and in another clime dream afresh the dream of life. But when I have fully ordered my business here, whither on a suddenness may I light on thee, Master Cromwell?"

"I will not be far from hence; send to me your present attendant. She hath the privilege of entrance to me at all seasons, and knoweth where to find me, forasmuch as she hath already approved herself a light amid the chosen Israel of our God," replied Cromwell. "But prithee be thou careful of thyself. Go not forth meanwhile from thy hiding-place, lest worse evil happen unto thee. To lie close here were the wisest mode and the safest, by my faith! Thou canst remain within the close-kept maze of these walls, as an thou wert already entombed amid the dead, where-among, by a strange luck-chance, thine enemies deem thou art about to be laid."

"How so, prithee, Master Cromwell?" asked Plantagenet, in some surprise.

"Why, thus. Believing thy wounds mortal,

they comfort themselves that thou art ere this past all human healing or further striving, and that, therefore, they have heard the last of thee," returned Cromwell, with a smile.

"Let them think so, an it please them. It little matters to me how falsely they delude themselves," remarked Plantagenet, with indifference.

"But such a fantasy worketh just now to thy good. See that thou spoil it not by appearing in thy robust mould without these walls, and amid the blazy light of day. I will to thee again ere another sun has set and risen, meanwhile I must begone, for other matters of grave and mighty import call me hence. Mind my caution, good youth, and fare thee well until at some future hour not far hence we yoke hands again."

So speaking, Cromwell departed. He had not, however, been long away, ere his thoughtful patient was visited by Raimond Verstegans, who, confident in his skill in the dismal branch of pharmacy, salved anew the many bruises of the young warrior monk, and administered unto him some of the posset-drink, which evidently contained an ingredient of an opiate nature, for ere long Plantagenet sank into a profound sleep which lasted out the better part of the remaining daylight hours. When towards the decaying of day he again awoke, he felt as one suddenly revived from death unto life, so thoroughly had the nervelessness of the muscles and the fevered heat of the blood departed, so amazingly reinvigorated and refreshed appeared his whole system. An hour of calm, peaceful thought quickly fled, as in the assured safety of his beloved and the bright hopes Cromwell's words had reawakened, his enamoured fancy dwelt with delight on the promised land of the future.

The day went down at last, and night spread her bespangled shroud over the darkened earth and the moonlit river. Richard Plantagenet in the end, wearying of the loneliness of his own thoughts and his dismal chamber, rose from his couch, and, donning his apparel as best he could amid the dusky tints of nightfall, strode to the window. As it was mild without, and the chamber appeared close within, he threw open the casement and looked forth on the wide expanse of starry blue—paling beneath the light of the advancing queen of night—hanging like a spangled canopy over the yellow glare of the even then vast city. Time fleeted by, another hour and yet another passed, as his restless thoughts beguiled the weary span of his solitude. He thought of his own grand descent and of the exquisite being whom his soul worshipped even in its desolation. And, combining the two, bitterly regretted for her sake his lost wealth, power, grandeur, and position. He remained thus lost for a considerable period, chain-locked by some dreamy mystic power, until at last, without warning, and despite his own active reasoning and sane opposition, a species of superstitious ague began to creep over him. His hair quickly hung heavy with drops of agitation, and he felt as if he stood in the actual presence of the great Œdipus—Death. He tried hard to shake off the phantasmal impression, and smiled dismally at his own fancies. He knew not that he was observed; that his every movement was intently watched; that in the impenetrable gloom of the far corner of his chamber, close beside the ancient arras of which her darkly dressed form appeared a part, stood the Maid of Kent. She seemed lost in some dreamy stupor as she intently searched into his every movement, while it indeed appeared as if she read the secrets of his thoughts in that long, profound, and melancholy gaze. She was for the time lost to all outward perception, while a single thought seemed frozen fixedly in her brain. There was something inexpressibly pleasing, something divinely attractive, in the doomed girl's expression and appearance. It might have been that her devotional observances, her intellectual employments, and the secret flame of her heart, had one and all completely asserted their powerful sway over the body; and hence on that eve her wild uncultivated beauty, her curbed soul beaming through her lustrous orbs, her almost seraphic looks, went far to realize, in her fixed immobility and the gloomy solitude of the ancient chamber, the form and attributes of a saint. At last the sudden chillness of some thought darker than the rest numbed her heart, and she sighed with unconscious heaviness. Plantagenet immediately turned round in inquiring wonder, not altogether unmixed with awe. Before, however, he could question further the cause of that moaning breath, the Maid herself approached.

"I have come, sir knight—I wish to say—what ails me? Beshrew me, I am so betossed by a sea of thoughts, that I know not what I would say," said she, tremulously, and with a lightning glance, which flashed through the heart of the Knight of St. John.

"Thou art welcome, Mistress Barton, most welcome; for my loneliness was becoming allnigh past bearance," said he, with kind consideration.

She paused for another minute beneath the force of an inward struggle, but the naked grandeur of natural feeling at last scorned the false drapery of artificial speech or movement, and it was with a strange vehemence she exclaimed :—

" Dan Theodulph was with thee early this morn. I overheard his mentionings of me, and how, with serpent-like cunning, he betrayed my soul to you. Yet—how shall I say it, that am ashamed to think it—his confession matters nothing now, dear knight; for, albeit I am wrong in thus doing, yet away I bid respect, and tell thee of myself, so that yon leprous monk shall not solely own the secret longer, that I love, nay, worship thee. He would vaunt it to thee for his own evil purposes, and, to perfect his plottings, trump up lies as big as Atlas. He always bethinks it wise to speak falsely if the mis-truth will hold good for an hour. Prithee, patience, dear youth, I will come to my point anon. I know what thou mayest urge, and that even thou wilt contend that love is solely a desire of the soul to mingle with another, to escape from a loneliness which otherwise might make of the earth's universe a vast and hopeless solitude, and that, as thou lovest another, there can be no return given by thee to the outspoken fervour of my soul. I seek it not. Let all the fire of thy noble nature be sacredly hoarded up for that sweet lady who is so fitting a recipient for it. Let the black treachery of father Theodulph pass by thee as a fierce gust of wintry wind. I have acknowledged, willingly and spontaneously, what he traitherously confessed to thee. Thou canst not blame me, in that I have not more securely kept captive my wandering soul. I will not pester thee with the glowing yearnings afire within me. Thou mayest of a surety meet me as heretofore without faltering or mislike. My time of tarriance on earth will soon be sped; —for oft, in my dreams, do I behold my end;— and, O God!—be merciful unto me, am self-warned that the dismal drama of my hapless existence speedily approaches a more fearful conclusion. Until that hour comes, still look kindly on the orphan girl; and when it has fully arrived, then befriend, in thought and feeling, the lone and friendless martyr on her transit to another world. Thy friendship needs not forsake me because I hold thee dearer than all humanity. Let it tarry with me yet awhile, and let it prove the angel to smooth my fiery pillow of death."

"You amaze me, Mistress Barton; and yet I cannot but feel pride at the warm interest thou entertainest for me," said the Knight of St. John, in some bewilderment, and then, in the kindly sympathy of his generous nature, adding, "Naught can I say of thee but what is well, and that there can be no sin in loving as thy loyal nature intends; for well I weet thou imaginest that, should all the power, wealth, and favour of this world fail to yield a single balmy impression of peace or comfort, the remembrance of even one good act breathes a perfume as sweet in the nostrils of death as flowerets to the lily Eve. But ever am I warned against, ever hear complaint of this dark friar. He speaketh smoothly, and ever discourseth

well and wisely.   Is he the repentant sinner he
himself affirms, or the specious hypocrite report
describes him ?"

" Dost not know, sir knight, that villany hath
a value in this world, albeit virtue hath none?
But quote me liar to the day of doom if I prove
not the sub-prior, Dan Theodulph, so black a
fiend that hell may even scruple to receive him.
He is working and toiling with slow and silent
cunning. We must, peradventure, deal with
him subtly, as with subtle men. His plot is
gradually cropping out of its secret darkness,
and will, anon, be broached to the light surface
of day. The hour is not yet, but, when it
comes, I'll unmask his projects, and lay bare his
dark scheming soul, ere he journeys to join the
eternal dead of hell. I will serve thee better
than thou canst conceive. There are still rocks
ahead of thy purposed course. The enemies
of thy peace sleep not, but are even now afoot
with other plans to mar the blissful visions of
thy heart."

" By the mass, what new evil hath happed,

or what further mischance dost thou believe foredoomed?" asked the Knight of St. John, anxiously, his mind immediately reverting to Aveline More, and suffering on the instant a racking chaos of fears and anticipations, not lessened or quieted by the next words of the Maid of Kent.

" Ay, ay, these are troublous and eventful times; and to keep apace with the age, it needeth we should be armed on all points," she exclaimed, with prophetic fervour. " I feel sorrowful, dear knight, I know not well why. Mayhap, coming death already casts its shadow on my path; or is it that some rare instinct warns me that danger to thee—thee—lurketh nigh? "

Poor soul! She would not penetrate too deeply the source of her sadness—that sadness which all nobler natures must feel when their high instincts and energies are wasted in a vain struggle to conquer the cruel phantom of hopeless love. The perfection of the young knight's person, his noble character, his chivalrous courage, and even his lineal haughtiness had all unitedly riveted her interest in the first days of their acquaintance. Her electric nature, surcharged as it was with suppressed sensibility and passion, had long been lying latent and ready on a moment to burst into flames at the first shock of the celestial bolt. She had confessed her passion well-nigh as soon as she herself had been aware of it. The malevolent disclosure of the sub-prior that very morn had avowed to herself the dangerous and irresistible frenzy of her soul. In her freedom of intercourse heretofore with the Knight of St. John, she had yielded without suspicion to the intoxicating pleasure of being in his presence—the only draught of bliss she had tasted for many weary years. The secret, albeit fatal spell had worked surely upon her, while the subtle magic of natural inclination aided its insidious advance. To her absorbed and charmed vision, the menaced danger of a hopeless passion appeared not to lurk in the bright hues of her sweet and happy dream—so terrible an antithesis as it proved to her destiny. She bent unconsciously towards the advancing fever, and the plague had stricken her ere she was scarce conscious of its presence. She had involuntarily permitted her soul to incline towards the idol of its native choice, nathedoubt subdued by the natural desire for sympathy—a need for which we are taught haunts even the broadest-winged spirit in its loftiest soar. All heretofore had been calm and peaceful, even amid the self-imagined dangers of her future life; and, while toiling persistently and laboriously in the service of the Eternal, she had not heeded the gliding of her bark amid the quicksands of Passion, or the danger of shipwreck on the rock of Love. But henceforth her reveries could be no longer the magnificent dreams of a cloudless and glory-bathing spirit—the stupendous hopes of a holy and martyred enthusiast. The fiend of Passion had trespassed within the bounds of the Eden of her imagination, and the whispering disclosures of the tempter had for ever tainted the sweetness and glory of her visionary world. She loved, therefore, the young Knight of St. John with all the frenzied fervour of a poetical inspiration, albeit conjointly with the warmth of an impassioned woman's heart. At her age, too, it was a feeling never to be effaced. She would carry it with her in her soul's holy of holies through life to the grave. She now felt her love, knew her danger, beheld the pitfall—dread, dark, and unfathomable; meanwhile well perceiving the temptation which beguiled her on to a degrading, albeit delicious ruin. She dared no longer in *his* presence question her secret thoughts, or further probe the furnace longings of her heart—no longer trust herself to the slightest exhibition of the mighty feeling within, lest the vast torrent, perceiving the slightest dam removed, should burst forth and overwhelm all. It was, therefore, with the intent to subdue the eager longings within her, and to school her troubled spirit against its hopeless aspirings, that she thought of one who successfully outrivalled her love, and, in somewhat dizzy accents, proceeded to make mention of her. In her anxiety to efface any unpleasant impression that her strange avowal may have excited, and to leave her memory still brightly impressed upon the heart of the Hospitaller, Elizabeth Barton displayed all her infinite charms of genius and beauty so profusely that, had not his whole soul been preoccupied, the intoxication of its pleasure must at last have assumed a species of pain in the unsatisfied yearning of the senses which were aroused.

"But it needs must be that I have become a very polypus of perverseness, sithence I thus lightly while time, when Innocence—which is, of a surety, like unto a dew-drop in the cup of a flower; touch it, it is lost for ever—may be battling, unfriended, against the remorseless power of lustful passion!" she exclaimed, as she suddenly ended her former converse and its emulous aspirings—the impulse of 'thoughts that wander through eternity,' and 'which in this world have but the two extremes, either steeping the soul in anguish or in bliss.

" By the mass! I pray thee tell me the import of thy fears. Thou hintest oft of some danger to be feared, and yet thou dost not disclose it, so that time and aidance may pervert or stay its progress. Have thy wits, Mistress Barton, gone a bell-wavering?" said Plantagenet, with a slight show of impatience.

"Thou art upon nettles, sir knight; but, credit me, nothing hath yet chanced to cause thee miseasiness," retorted the Maid of Kent, in a hesitating tone, and with a slightly bitter accent. A struggle of a moment sufficed to control the unruly impulse, and, in a calm and gentle manner, with a wavering, wooing smile that it seemed impossible to resist, she continued—"Thou wouldst know full fain what of evil omen lurks beneath the night gloom for thee and for the gentle lady thou lovest so well. They work at night who dread the piercing eye of day, and think to lead captive beneath the dusky robe the matchless mine of allurement that Mistress More hath buried in her untutored charms. Let them labour, let them plot; the more enlisted to their side the greater chance, I may avow, of miscarriage. They shall not, howsoever, work their enginery to elude my craft, albeit they labour as darkly as the moles. And yet if it be that the king is gained to their cause, what further hope have we?"

These last words were uttered in a dreamy, ruminating tone; but, quick as light, they flashed a new cause of fearful anxiety upon Richard Plantagenet's mind, while increasing to fever-heat his wild impatience.

"The king,—say you? Prithee what hath such a belly-god to do with Aveline More? Will he venture, think you, to cross anew my path? If he doth, by all the saints, I will smite him as though he were the veriest carrion of humanity!" exclaimed the Knight of St. John, with furious vehemence.

"Thine ancient enmity against the Tudor race doth blind thy reason, dear knight, or thou wouldst know that Henry, the bloodthirsty and ruthless, will permit no protection, no power, scarce the grave itself, to keep aught he desires from fulfilment or from his own violent clutch. He hath, too, the power and force of the whole realm to back him and to do his pleasure, against which, how canst thou, a single knight, hope to strive? But Heaven shall show thee, Richard Plantagenet, how a woman can love in all purity and faith, and how crush to remorseless atoms the blighted but glowing sensation. Come with me now, follow me closely through the intricacies of this spacious castle, and I will show thee the secret things of darkness amid the mazy ways of this stolid, time-proven building."

She strode to the end of the chamber, beside the spot where first we remarked her presence, a while agone. She paused for the Hospitaller to approach, and then, lifting the arras, pressed one hand against what appeared a solid panel in the dark oak behind, and immediately a secret door receded slowly back, displaying a low and narrow archway, of pitchy impenetrable depth. Taking one hand of the wondering knight she entered the gloomy passage, and drawing him within closed to the well-constructed door. She then advanced, piloting the way down, what seemed a narrow but long inner corridor, for a considerable distance, and then, turning suddenly to the right, ascended several steps, which brought them to another secret passage on a higher level. The light which streamed through several eyelet holes on the left hand side, begat a pleasant interval to the opaque darkness they had penetrated, and were again entering. Looking through one of these holes, the Hospitaller perceived they were traversing, at a high altitude, the length of the great hall of the castle, which could be well discerned in all its noble proportions and knightly garnishings of bannerols, swords, pikes, axes, and shields by the light of the moon, whose beams poured streaming in through the high clerestory windows on the further side. Pursuing their dark and silent way, they descended, on arriving at the further end of the hall, once more to the lower level. Proceeding a few yards further, they again descended some

half-dozen steps, and then, after traversing a
level of some twenty yards, and after coiling
round within a passage so narrow that they
were obliged to walk singly—a passage evidently
traced within the walls of one of the great
towers—they suddenly emerged on to the top
of a well-staircase, up which a cold, damp air
came fanningly. They were obliged to proceed
with caution down these steps, for they were
slimy and slippery with moisture. Having
reached the bottom, they started along another
passage wide enough to allow the explorers to
stretch their arms at full length, and unevenly
floored with chalk and sand, amid which their
footsteps fell noiselessly. The Maid informed
the knight their way now lay beneath the main
yard of the castle, and, having reached the
further side, they again ascended a winding
stair similar to that they had so shortly before
descended. But instead of pursuing the straight
passage which led off from this tower on the
same level as the one they had previously quitted,
they continued to wind round and round the

giddy turnings of the spiral stairs, until they reached what appeared to be a small recess. Into this the Knight of St. John plunged in pursuit of the Maid of Kent, but was the next moment stayed by an opposing wall, and, as he gazed down with wild interest and excitement upon it through a large eyelet hole, enthralled by a scene as powerfully interesting as any that could be imagined for a young, loving and adventurous spirit such as his—a scene that held him spell-bound, as though beneath some enchanter's wand.

CHAPTER XIV.

Ţhe Chamber of Otranto.

THE belief in magic and necromancy throughout the dark ages was general. A craving
after prophecies, a desire to invoke spirits, an
eager searching into the unholy of unholies, a
restless avidity to pry into the hidden darkness
of the future by abnormal means, infected,
more or less, all ranks, from the highest to the
lowest.   The antique science of rhabdomancy,
or the divining by wands; the dæmonology of
the ancient Chaldeans; the shadowy lucubrations of the old Scandinavian Valas, or witches,
of the less remote Boudhists and dervishes of
Arabia, and even of the later Obi of the
Africans; the cabala of the Jewish doctors;
the mystical leaves of the sibyls; and the
divers magic phenomena propounded by other

masters of the occult sciences of chiromancy, astrology, and soothsaying, found innumerable devout and earnest disciples, who were, one and all, eager to search into the wonders of the preternatural, to invoke spectral visitations from shadowland, or to behold the mystic prognostications of the Dim Unknown.

As instances of this universal credulity even amid the highest circles, we find that Anne Boleyn blessed a basin of rings, her royal fingers pouring such virtue, as it was believed, into the metal that no disorder could resist it.* Wolsey possessed and highly prized a consecrated magic crystal; while Cromwell, the famous secretary and sceptic, " did haunt to the company of a wizard."†

Raimond Verstegans was not of that common herd of magicians who had for so many ages abounded in every city, town, and hamlet, and who were but, at the best, ingenious jugglers. He was an earnest cultivator of that mystic lore,

* Burnet's Collectanea, p. 355.   † Rolls House MS.

which tradition asserts was one of the principal studies in the colleges and among the priesthood of the ancient world. He had read deeply, studied laboriously, and had acquired fame in physiology, pathology, alchemy and all the obtuse sciences of the age. He had acquired each solemn secret which lays hidden within the cabalistic ring of the nobler or theurgic magic—a magic, the existence of which, at one period in this world's history, it is well not altogether to disbelieve, for assuredly it is not easy to disprove—an art or a science not open wholly to competition, and but rarely acquired —a study that was wholly distinct from the paltry commodity of the impostor, and one which, we may suppose, more nearly assimilated that chronicled so oft in Holy Writ.

Within the chamber of this learned man, and upon which, while the bells of the monastery were tolling forth the witching hour, the unseen inquisitors looked down, were all the strange fittings and weird-like appointments we have described in a previous chapter. A large moveable brazier, filled with charcoal, from which sprang powerful innocuous flames, as of some hidden nourishment, cast a preternatural and almost terrible aspect upon the necromantic surroundings. From a hook in the centre of the roof depended a large globe of crystal glass, filled with some pure pellucid liquid, and in which, describing perpetual gyrations, floated a small snake, like the chameleon of ever varying hue. On the centre table were divers stillatories at work, with alembics and other instruments of glass. Beside the brazier was perched a curiously constructed chest, the lid of which stood open, disclosing manifold divisions, nathedoubt containing such ingredients as were needful for the proper administration of the occult science. Whether among them were the mandrake apple's rind, the recipe of Ernestus Burgranius, the curled hair of a wolf's tail prescribed by the sage Mizaldus, a swallow's liver, the dust of a dove's heart, or the scrapings from the ass's hoof propounded by the learned Rebens, we know not, for the chronicler relateth it not.

Within the recess formed by the bowed-window stood the figure of Raimond Verstegans, looking like a Druid sage, with his rich embossed garb, his leathern girdle covered by mystic hieroglyphics, and a consecrated beryl hanging from his neck, which, by its dimness, it was averred, faithfully forewarned him of any impending danger. He was engrossed in some experiment of grave and anxious import, which he was carefully attesting upon Aveline More, who reclined upon a high back settle close beside, so calm and so sepulchral looking that she e'en resembled a marble chiselling of Repose. Already had the beauteous girl lost her elasticity of form, together with the colour and mien of health, through a sudden, secret and all corroding sorrow. She was plainly, albeit neatly attired in a sacque of blue Florence silk, tied with a tassel round her waist. Upon both, through the open casement of the uncurtained window, were the fairy rays of the vesper lamp of night—the full moon—beaming, lighting up all that the blazing brazier failed to illuminate. Apart, within the shadow formed by the massive, gathered-up arras, which was at night-time usually lowered before the large window recess, stood one, in whose pallid countenance and basilisk eyes the observant Maid of Kent at once recognised the features of the sub-prior, and thereupon so intimated to her enthralled companion. Amid the unearthly glare of the flaming brazier, Dan Theodulph resembled one consumed by some fierce internal fire, while his eyes glowed and glared darkly as the flames of a lime-kiln by night. And well might it be so, oppressed as was his soul with feelings which worked banefully on the fancy, while deafening the conscience and imperilling the soul.

The deep, impressive tones of Raimond's voice broke the dread silence of night and chamber.

" The life of man," he said, " is like unto a sparrow flitting in at one window of the festal chamber, and out at another—it springs from the Great Darkness and it flees back to the Great Darkness. But in thy case, sweet lady, the flame of light which sped heavenward in thy childhood, returns again to thee in thy youth. Glory be to Thee, Most High !"

" Oh !—what,—what is this blessed scene ? What are those dim outlines looking so far off ? What this gleaming stream beneath ?—and oh, what that round light subdued, floating in mid-heaven ?" exclaimed the lovely girl starting up, and, in her excessive agitation, trembling violently, as she clasped together her small white hands, and gazed through the open casement upon the fairy moonlit scene, and up to the sky where rode the wan lamp of night, and where sparkled the distant worlds.

" The high hills, the glistening river, the lesser light, are the real objects that, in thy restored vision, thy ravished sight so blissfully embraces. 'Let there be light, and there was light,' was one of the divine mandates of Creation; let there be light, is still the desire of thy God, even to the humblest of his creatures. To Him, therefore, unto the great I Am of whom the whole universe is so full, give thanks, for unto

Him alone is the honour due," exclaimed the ancient oculist with impressive fervour.

The beauteous lady, rejoicing in her sight restored, albeit all happiness seemed fled; grateful for the interposition of Providence, despite the worse loss with which it had been pleased to afflict her, sank down upon her knees, and lifting up her clasped hands, like some wakeful vestal at her holy shrine, poured forth a solemn, fervent thanksgiving, which, while her tearful eyes fixed their first intelligible glance on heaven's purple vault, and those brilliant planets—stupendous worlds, to human ken no larger than the glowworm's lamp—she doubted not in her pure and simple faith, was heard and recorded by the Great Seer of all. She arose from her knees, still doubting, still wondering that, having been so long and so wearyingly afflicted, Heaven had really thrice blessed her by restoring her vision. The blissful reality which had for so many weeks seemed nigh, for such long days and nights prayed for and sighed for, from peep of day until russet

eve, had in deed and very truth come at last
to pass. Having given thanks to the Mighty
Father of all good blessings, she turned around
to re-echo her grateful feelings to her human
operator ; but he had already quitted the recess,
and was poring over some of the mazy, mystic
scrolls of Time and Futurity, which lay amid the
miscellaneous strewments of the great centre
table. She approached, she knelt on one knee
beside the noble figure of this second Sydrophel,
and, taking one worn, fevered hand in hers, she
pressed it fervently to her lips.

"To thee, good, kind attendant on my late
long infirmity, are my next best thanks most
fully due," she exclaimed, with a grace not the
less winning because it partook, in a slight
degree, of the embarrassment of awe.

"Thank me not, gentle child. I have but
done my duty, and am already repaid," he
answered benignantly, and then, while something of solemn and prophetic darkness gathered
over his noble countenance, he added as he
faced his late patient, and gazed earnestly at

her, " Venus is, I perceive, malefic—but the hyleg* is not afflicted. An evil influence hath crossed thy heart-worship, and further danger is threatened thee. Tell me more of thyself—thy secret self. The dark heavings of human consciences oft cast their sultry plannings up to my appraisement. I may, peradventure, be able to forewarn thee, ere yet too late."

" Oh! speak not of it, messire. My trouble, my sorrow, and even my newly-restored vision, matter little now, sithence I am about to eschew the world, and seek peace and solace within some cloistral haven," answered Aveline tearfully, still foredeeming naught but woe and fortune's frown.

" Nay, dear child, such surely cannot be thy own heartfelt wish or well-matured intent!" remonstrated Raimond Verstegans with a doubting smile.

" I attest in the presence of God's infinite goodness, in the sight of his glorified Mother,

* Astrological term signifying " Giver of life."

and the whole blissful court of Heaven, such to be
my intention, such my earnest desire, such my
firm resolve," retorted Aveline in woful earnestness, for Hope's wild raptures thrilled no
more her soul.

"There is more here than strikes outward
observance," said the learned astrologer in
thoughtful self-commune, and, after a moment's
pause, adding aloud, "But, prithee, tell me the
name of thy lover. Of a surety he cannot be
so unworthy, sithence so lustrous and fair a
soul as thine did choose him. Yet it matters
not—in the starry shade of night I learn the
language of another world, and I can read it
here." And again he turned to the table, and
pored over the outspread scroll. A silence both
dread and exciting then followed—a silence un-
disturbed by each one of those engrossed and
interested spectators. Even Dan Theodulph
moved not, spoke not, but remained as one
spell-bound, albeit the coming revelation might
unmask and altogether undo him.

In about five minutes, Raimond Verstegans

again spoke, though still intently perusing the mystical plan of human destiny stretched out before him with its emblazoned figures surrounded by the signs of the zodiac. "I can plainly discern thy track of light through the measureless future; and, though evil besets thee, I can predict for thee no such mischance as thy own ill-advised intent doth augur of. Thou lovest, gentle lady, the last branch of a once mighty tree," he added as he turned around.

"I must needs acknowledge I did. Ay, noble Raimond, I loved him well, with no weak impoverished flame, for my very heart-strings were twined with his, and I would have died as many deaths as could be well devised, ere I had been false to him in the poor tittle of but one smile that should have been his," the simple girl sobbingly confessed.

"Why droop then now like a trampled lily. Thou shalt live to see that the stars are mightier than the despairing throes of a young maiden's heart. For the signs and portents of the celestial hemisphere announce that, in spite of thy present wanhope, thou shalt be his—he thine—both evermore one the other's, while fame, glory, peace and love shall, star-like, gem your skies. Bright love shall be your dowry—proud honour his inheritance. Be thou therefore comforted, dear child; for a far more exalted than I hath decreed that, amid the silent years of time, thus it shall be with ye twain."

But all would not do, a deep, foreboding gloom hung like a night-pall over her spirits, over her best hopes. Suspicion, thrice damned, had been forced into her once all-trusting heart, lies black as that of Atlas had tainted and discoloured the honour and the faith of her soul's idol. The insidious and hell-spawned words of Dan Theodulph, " He will be evermore to you as but a distant star, whose cold light beams upon thee the colder for its far aloof brilliancy," still rankled in her captivated soul; while to her thus seemingly wrecked existence, to this changed flow in the tide of her destiny, she yielded amid the exhaustion of lost hope and newly-acquired despair.

"Eighteen summers have scarce flown over your young head, dear child; but winters three-score and ten have sown their snows on mine. You have yet to learn that, while years have ploughed wrinkles on my face, they have brought wisdom to my mind. Know thee that to struggle with fate is to wrestle with Omnipotence. Thy destiny is foreseen, hath through me been foretold. 'Tis no fancy donning the garb of truth. Thou canst not avert it; therefore, doubt not, neither despond. But though I have enow on hand to last me out the night stars; yet let me look again, for I may perchance be able to warn thee of the threatening evil, and enlighten thee of the dark shadow, which it would beseem lurketh ever beside thee, instilling its poison and leaving its sting." And once more he became engrossed in the spiritual cabala, while once more a dread silence lurked around, and while once more a common engrossment of all the amazed and wondering auditors thereupon ensued.

Ere he could complete his fresh research, ere he could, by forewarning her, save Aveline a world of misery and despair, ere expose the wily serpent that glided softly in the hedge-rows of her life's-path, a sudden and discordant rush of voices, the trampling and shuffling of many feet, announced a numerous approach. The next moment the stout oaken door was thrown wide, and in marched a small cohort of gaudily-attired mummers. A tall, burly and haught personage, closely masked, and attired in a rich gown of damask furred with miniver, a white satin doublet and hose of russet velvet, led the way, followed quickly by a throng re-sembling the gaudy escort of an Eastern Satrap. The arrivals included that strange and hateful admixture of deceit and ferocity, wild inconti-nence and savage pride, Henry the Eighth, the new privy councillor Sir Thomas Cromwell, Sir John Perrot, and his shadow Sir Ralph Sadler, Sir William Brereton, Lord Rochfort,

Sir Henry Norris, and some minor courtiers, the comrades of the king's jovial hours, with several trusty attendants.

A shadowy crimson stole over Aveline's face, as she gazed, in the plenitude of her newly-acquired vision, with wild and misdoubting confusion at the sudden incursion and at the motley arrivals. Dan Theodulph was the first to recover from the general surprise, and breaking at once the strange spell by which he had hitherto appeared rooted to one spot, he started forward, and, seizing the lovely girl by one fairy-rounded arm, he drew her aside, muttering in her ear, " This is no longer a fitting tarriance for thee, daughter, amid such troublesome roysterers. We must away as secretly as may be ; meanwhile list ye not to the airy bubbles of a mad astrologer's raving. We will bide in the shadow until we can scape the notice of this presence." But other eyes had already descried them, and they were not doomed to quit the chamber without attention or obstruction. Sir John Perrot—who ever had before him the sweet girl's gentle eyes, which drooped, and her little coral mouth, which trembled, whenever his bold speech fell upon her ear—at once perceived them.

Raimond fixed an earnest though calm glance of enquiry on each one of the intruders, seeming to pierce, as his eyes passed from one to the other, the frail disguise of the shapeless mask and gaudy garniture.

The royal but bloated Bluebeard was the first among the unwelcome arrivals to speak, as in a loud, imperious, albeit mocking tone, he thus apostrophized the renowned astrologer—" We poor night-wanderers have penetrated to thy presence Master Raimond, to seek from thee the marrow of certain things hidden. Therefore will it please you, great Magian—genius of romantic awe—to avise us what is now in the ascendant, and who is lord of the conjunction. Doth the meeting of Saturn and the Moon in Scipio argue ill? What, too, saith Jovianus? Hath Mercury fled to the arms of Virgo, or hath Pisces stumbled into the path of Mars? Speak to us, most learned pundit, by the mystery of thy spells, some shuddering tale of goblins pale. Being wayfarers from afar, and hearing much of thy fame, we have steered our courses hither as best we might, to learn from thee some wrinkles of our future lives, albeit not looking for any mystery which needeth blood to seal."

"The voice of the thunder, the glare of the lightning, and the howl of the hurricane, should announce to Henry of England that the gods, though far above the burning zone, are enwrothed, and that he should tremble for crimes unrepented of in the past, for the blood-guilty existence threatening him in the future!" said Raimond, in a stern, impressive manner.

"Hoity-toity! The wizard hath unmasked us; but methinks he must needs be drunken with wine, to venture thus in our presence to utter such disloyal catches, albeit we may prove the very myrmidons of fate," retorted the king in angry amaze.

"The stars, though to human vision number-less in their distinct glory, form but one galaxy

of beauty in the sight of the Eternal, while
shedding a common light on this dark waste of
earth and waters," said Raimond, with impassioned grandeur. " So, amid the millions of
earth, the Creator beholds all as but one fold,
under one common shepherd, who is enabled to
discern, with an instant's flash, the black amid
the white of the flock, and furthermore sums up,
in but one long reckoning, the manifold errors
and crimes of a whole lifetime. Thy future, as
well as thy past, O king, is known unto me,
albeit through no angel-breath of revelation.
Seek not to unravel that which hath naught of
good in its colouring or aspect. Depart from
me, but mark well my words—The benison for
the slaughtered, the ban for the destroyer, the
withering curse for the despoiler, will ascend
before thy death to the God of thy fathers.
The tyrant who depriveth his victims of all
hope, but sharpens the dagger for his own foul
breast; and, despite thine own dark opposings,
the flame of liberty shall yet be kindled on
some mountain top, to pervade the whole land

as of old the brightness shone on Sinai. I have spoken—and will no more." And he turned aside to continue the astrological investigation in which he had been engaged ere thus unwelcomely interrupted.

The king gazed with features distorted by sudden passion at the noble form of Raimond Verstegans, as it stood out in bold relief between the royal party and the lapping flames of the brazier furnace; but the words of wrathful menace died away upon his lips, subdued by a superstitious awe he could neither explain nor drive away. The attendant courtiers were equally amazed, though perchance not equally disconcerted.

" What!—are ye all struck dumb, like parrots in a thunderstorm, at this Magian's mad rudeness? 'Twas a foolish emprise, and our court fools will make a rare jest of it. So, my lords, we will e'en depart as we came, and leave this Astaroth in his dismal hell, and to his own weird hatchings," exclaimed the king, with enforced composure, as he turned in high dudgeon to depart.

" I cry you mercy, a moment pause, my noble sire ! Thou canst do me a service here," said Sir John Perrot impatiently, while interposing and pointing to where still stood, like a blushing saint, the berayed but closely veiled Aveline.

" Ha ! By St. George, whom have we here ?" exclaimed the king, eager on a new scent.

" My redoubted lord, 'tis no other than she you wot of, the noble lady I brought to thy presence at the tournay, and for whom I bespoke your interference yestreen," answered Sir John Perrot, as he gazed disturbedly and with a strange admixture of love and passion, upon the beauteous girl. He could not analyze his strange and perverse partiality for her, while his sudden engrossment of her beauty had been nursed in that rash and obstinate spirit with which he had ever plunged into fresh amours or exciting adventures. In the wandering existence he had pursued for so many a year, his career had been one of such fanciful vagary, and such wild danger, that his code of morality fitted him at last as loosely as the robes of a monk. He always answered the tauntings of his friends by asserting he was fully alive to the folly that a man like unto himself would commit by tying himself in marriage to one dame, however illustrious and beautiful, like a love-knot to a woman's kirtle. He had, too, questioned himself of late in secret rather more closely. Indeed, so late as on the morn preceding this unpremeditated eve-meeting, he had held solitary self-communion much after this fashion—"Springs this powerful leaning from any fathomable source? Doth her beauty subdue me? I have beheld as beautiful. Is it her air of simple dignity, or her display of melancholy but natural pride? Have I not met and known the haughtiest damsels of Europe. Then, what can it be?" He could not perceive that nameless something which, in the path of every man, fixes once during his lifetime his sole real affection upon an object ofttimes the furthest removed, the most inaccessible.

the

" Ha!—say you so? Welcome, lady!" exclaimed Henry. " But how comes it we find her in this weirdman's abode ?"

At this moment the sub-prior stood forward, thinking to interpose between our heroine and further displeasant notice, and on behalf of her more certain quick escapement from all courtly or other espial.

" Mistress More hath been brought hither under my guidance, messire, and hath, after a most miraculous manifestation, had her blindness anointed with Jesu's quickening spittle, the result whereof hath been, that, like the blind of old, the black scales have fallen from her eyes, and, our Lady be praised, she can now behold all things as in a glass, face to face," he said, in humble tones.

" Ha!—say you so? And did our Magian yonder effect this marvellous cure," said the king, in a wondering undertone, and again regarding Raimond's still closely engrossed form with awe-like astonishment.

" Even so, my liege!" answered the sub-prior,

" and, furthermore, he did caution her very earnestly 'gainst a too long tarriance in the night air, and so we will, sire, with your good pleasure, retire, in order that she may seek the rest and solitude so needful for her bodily weal.

" Let me remind your grace that our newly exalted queen did express a wish to have this gentle lady amid her starry train, and beshrew me, good my father, thou didst so promise her," urged Sir John Perrot, as he roused himself once more from his soul-struck reverie.

" Ay, troth,—so did I ; and by St. George, we will in all things see the wishes of our most Heavenly Blisse made law, in these rare jocund hours !" said Henry, with his usual boisterous impetuosity.

" Although, my liege, it is widely affirmed that court favour is a bird of an early moult, I should have advised Mistress More to conform to your gracious intimation, an it had pleased her own leanings ; but for her own peace's sake she must no more mingle amid the gaieties of the world. She is pure in spirit even as the angels of God are pure, and is as yet the innocent betrothed of our most holy Lord, who hath in the gracious miracle vouchsafed unto her this eve, shown His acceptance of her," urged the sub-prior with devout earnestness.

"Ho!—by my fay, an such be the case, son Perrot, we cannot interpose as an we would have wished! So, monk, let our Lady keep well your penitent in her blessed and virginal purpose," exclaimed Henry. "Nay, look not so down in the muzzle, son Perrot, we will give thee other and better game for wifeage. So be comforted, sweet wench, thou shalt have thy will, howe'er untowardly chosen, and shalt thereby ensure thy safety from all ensnaring devices. But what further seekest thou of us, dan monk, sithence thou still continuest to crook thy humble-knee to us."

"I do beseech a short private audience of thee, my liege. I have matter of infinite moment for your royal hearing," answered the sub-prior in a wavering undertone.

"What's ado? Thou art not, methinks, a good intelligencer, sithence thou croakest like a ghost from a hollow tree. But we will hear thee, an thou makest thy narrative short," said the king, advancing a few yards in front of his followers.

Meanwhile Sir John Perrot proceeded to the side of Aveline More, and paid anew his unwelcome court to her.

"Oh, gentle lady, may it please you to pause ere you thus wantonly blight a heart that loves thee, and darken evermore thine own existence, by mewing thy precious person in a living tomb! Thy beetle-browed confessor, who, mayhap, is seduced by the devil, and hath methinks, little of the fear of God before his eyes, if all be true that the many tales concerning him assert, urges thee on in furtherance of his own evil devices, and to thy own bewrayment," said he, speaking thickly, as if half choked by some overwhelming emotion.

"It wearies me to hear thee talk thus, messire. Will no answer save me from thy

further persecution. Hark, you, sir!—and I
pray you let my refusal be for once and for ever.
Sooner than be the thing thou wouldst so foully
make me, I would cheerfully bear all that
poverty hath of contempt or lowliness of
bitterness, as the wedded bride of the man I
esteemed, though he were the poorest beggar,
or the most abject unfortunate, that ever gazed
upon the sun in his despair, to shun its light
and to curse its warmth," she replied with an
earnestness and a significance there was no
mistaking, while her face was carnationed with
the hues of virgin modesty.

"Meseems thou altogether wrongest me,
sweetest dulcibelle, and misdoubtest mine intent. The lightning of thy being, seraph queen,
hath quickened anew mine heart. I do but
seek thee now, most lustrous of thy sex, in all
lawfulness, and would make thee my peerless
wife before the world and all mankind. This—
and this only do I urge on thy acceptance, lady
—naught else, by my troth, and as knighthood
and honour be my meed," said Sir John Perrot,

kneeling in the adoration of his frenzied passion, while fervently seizing her hand, and pressing it to his lips.

"Nay, I pray you, sir, not to single me out thus notedly before men's eyes. You honour me, I will endeavour to believe, by your preference, but it cannot be ; were it even otherwise possible, my heart is no longer my own to give. Nay, in all beseechance, rise sir, and let me pass. See, his grace the king looks hither-ward," she urged, in inexpressible alarm and simplicity, while a heart-heaving sigh convulsed her fairy frame.

"Come, my lords, we will away, and leave this reverend man to outwatch the stars and to hatch his crocodile's egg, without the sun of our favour," cried the king, as he returned to the attendant group and prepared to depart.

" Oh, sire, treat not so lightly these murmurings of the coming storm, else, perchance, it may prove thy evil destiny to behold the Church—the antique and only Church—rent in twain, and a chasm opened down which countless generations, perishing eternally, shall fall into the abyss," urged Dan Theodulph, in support of some arguments he had been impressing on Henry.

"I know all that thou wouldst urge, gossip; so prithee spare thyself and us. The Maid—the nun, or the woman, howe'er she styleth herself—you speak of hath ere this had a warning from us; let her look to it, or perchance worse occasion may come of it," answered the king, impatiently. "But hark, my lords! Did ye not hear a noise—a rustle in the tapestry up yonder—a something like a footstep? Let us haste from hence ere we are all bewitched by some outlandish adjurations," and he turned in somewhat undignified haste to depart. But on the moment a loud, imperious voice bade him—even him—tarry.

"Stay, Henry of England—stay!" exclaimed Raimond Verstegans, of a sudden raising himself to his full height, and sternly regarding the somewhat dismayed king. "Dost thou think to ride upon the coming storm as an thou wert the Magus raising it ? I know not whom thou wouldst uncharnel. But ere now thou didst ask for some signs to be given thee. Tarry where thou art for a little span, and peradventure these signs shall be shown unto thee."

CHAPTER XV.

The Shadows on the Wall.

" WE will pleasure ourselves by obeying thine enjoining, Master Raimond; the more so sithence we have come hither on this very pretence, and, furthermore, not desiring to scurry from thy presence like scalded dogs. So we will e'en tarry a while, despite all annoy, and in full trust thou wilt not bewitch us with charmed drugs; but that thou wilt wield the wand of science to our enlightenment," exclaimed Henry, with an effort to appear calm and indifferent, albeit an insupportable ache of a sudden seized upon his heart.

His courtiers and attendants, in full expectation of some visible and fearful manifestation, gathered around his royal person, in eager and anxious amaze. Meanwhile Dan Theodulph was prevented leaving with his precious charge by the interposition of Sir John Perrot and Sir Ralph Sadler; and thus, with his anxious penitent, became an interested spectator of the mysteries, beyond the span of human ken, that were to be revealed—of the new '*Clamor ad Deum*' about to be repeated to kingly ears.

Raimond paid no attention to other proceedings, or to the curiosity of his engrossed auditors. He went about his preparations, wholly enthralled in the solemn predictions and spiritual manifestations he sought to invoke. He rolled the flaming brazier, which moved on noiseless wheels, to the front of the large antique-shaped mirror we have described in a previous chapter. At a motion of his hand, the dark curtain that was drooped before the reflecting surface silently rose, the brazier dimmed its light to a sullen glow, leaving all else but its own immediate surface in impenetrable darkness as the arras fell before the window, shutting out the glaring of the midnight moon. He then placed a chafing dish upon the ruddy charcoal, wherein for some seconds he kept carefully dropping several mystical compounds—the rescripts of grey tradition. As these ingredients began to ignite in an unearthly glow, the Magian regarded intently a page of an Oriental manuscript rarely illuminated with magic signs and configurations.

In a minute's span he looked up, and without turning, addressed, in a low, impressive voice, the following words of warning : " The slumber of ebon night now lies on the surface of the earth, and on the face of the waters ; and I know not what may be the sign about to be given unto thee, O king. Whether it shall appear as a Gabriel with warning hand, or as an Iblis with glowing finger hot from hell, I cannot predicate. But bide where ye now are ; seek not a nigher approach, unless ye would take a fearful danger by the gorget. There are weapons of destruction in the arsenal of the Omnipotent, we on earth wot not of. Most commonly he speaketh unto us in the earthquake, the storm, and the manifold convulsions of the world ; but more seldom do we hear his footfall, and perceive his pointing hand, in some direct spiritual manifestation—made unto those like unto thee, O king, who demand a sign and need a warning—like the renewed thunderings and blazings of Sinai!"

" God's saints! I know not how to answer thee on this matter, sithence I still hold some doubts of thy power to summon spirits from Paradise or Hades, or to foredeem aright our horoscope," said the king, with unusual hesitation.

" Ay, ever is it so! Mortals deem everything impossible that seems beyond the power of humanity, measuring all they image solely by their own limited capacities. What spirit, then, wouldst thou have summoned? Whose form of corruption wouldst thou uncharnel?"

" Had I the sleeve of Hildebrand, from which he shook out thunder and lightning, I would answer thee, show me the whole array of mine enemies; but, by St. George and St. Denis, having solely my sceptre and kingly will, I must

content me with a peep into futurity ! Show
me our newly bedded queen, and let her take
any form save that of the present darkness,
which methinks ill suits all creation save hell's
haughty king."

" Thou hast spoken. Be silent—be wary;
for thy request is about to receive some super-
nal divulgment," said Raimond, in a low hurried
tone.

The fumes from the chafing dish suddenly
emitted a dense white vapour, which rolled
slowly and sullenly upward, spreading out over
the entire surface of the magic mirror, and
lighting it up with a pale, mystic glow. The
vapour in a second or two seemed to roll back
on either side, leaving in the centre a small
surface of the glass clearly defined, wherein re-
flected, appeared a luminous figure, standing out
in bold and sharp outline, like unto the Scin-
Læca, or shining corpse, of the Scandinavian
legends, whose pale visage and shadowy form
resembled, in marvellous duality, those of Anne
Boleyn, the newly created queen. The eyes of the

beautiful phantom looked piercingly at Henry, and with so ominous a glare as well-nigh curdled to ice his heart's blood. Gradually becoming more distinct, came forth beside it a black block and a glittering weapon—the heads-man's axe—while a perceptible change came over the features of the spectral figure, which assumed all the frigid and appalling symptoms of death's chilly hue, while a gory stream was seen weltering from the fair rounded neck. The vapour rolled back again and the vision was gone.

While the whole of the auditors stood in marvelling amaze, and with breathless awe, while a fearful chill seized each quaking heart, the king's flushed countenance had grown white as Death's pale horse, his teeth were clenched, his eyes stared wildly and fixedly forward, while his wavy locks became drenched in the dark sweat which streamed down his face.

" Is it with dread of the future or fear for the past, thou sinkest dismayed, O King, at this visitation from out the night of ages !" demanded

the solemn voice of the Magian amid the darkness wherein he stood.

"Proceed in thy phantasmal lucubrations.
Shake the universe with thy weird spells an
thou pleasest, but let my soul be further assured
or it will burst in this expectant silence," gasped
the king in horror-stirring amaze.

"It needs not I should read you the fearful
doom foreshadowed her whom now you charm
with thy basilisk enticements. Hath not the
luminous shadow spoken unto thee with its
tongueless voice? Is not the presaging of Fate
therein more eloquent than an army of denounc-
ing words? But still other foredoomings are
about to be revealed unto thee which it would
be well for thee, O king, not to slight," said
Raimond impressively, as he again supplied some
rare chemicals to the glowing dish.

Once more the vapour arose, white and luminous as before, once more spreading out over
the whole mirror, once more parting midway,
and once more revealing a spectral figure robed
in filmy gauze, and looking unsubstantial almost

as the mist; in whose facial lineaments and outlines of form, the bedazed observants easily traced those of Jane Seymour, one of the maids of honour to the newly-made queen. This apparition bore in her arms an infant boy, upon whom it gazed in rapt melancholy, and as it did so, there came over its unsubstantial features all the revolting semblances of Death's last swoon, and then it faded gradually away like a dissolving view, while in its place, another female shadow in a few seconds' time stood as luminously revealed. A broken chain lay at its feet, symbolic of disruption in married life. That, too, faded, and another quickly followed. In this case were repeated the dread symbolic devices of a violent death, already foreshadowed in the vision of Anne Boleyn. In turn, this spectrum dissolved, but yet another took its place, whose unsubstantial accessories were of a more numerous and intricate nature. To the left of the mirror, and in its rear, the clouds of mephitic vapour formed themselves into a species of couch, upon which lay a figure as

luminous as the rest, but in whose burly form
and bloated features all present, in an instant's
flash, recognized the king.   Upon this spectral
shadow were concentrated the horror-fascinated
eyes of all, as they beheld it writhe like a serpent
in its coils, covered as it was by certain yellow
excrescences and green ooze, which started
forth from its surface amid the throes of living
corruption.   And while it lay thus in seeming
mortal agony, the four previous luminous
shadows gradually reappeared, conjointly with a
majestic fifth, whose noble lineaments were the
perfect reflex of the Lady Catharine's, and all of
whom, together with the sixth shadow of the
present scene, flitted slowly around the couch of
hideous mortality, pointing ever, with avenging
purpose, at the mass of corruption, and at a
dusk and awful figure that rose, like an infernal
god, from out of nothing—the grim outline of
Death sitting beside the misty pillow.   With a
strange, horror-freezing wail, half despair half
triumph, the dread apparition slowly dissolved,
as the cloudy vapour rolled back once more,

shutting out all from the sight of those who had been looking aghast at the spectral throng.

The chafing-dish was removed, and the dim lurid flames of the brazier reappeared, announcing the fearful incantation to have reached an end.

"Speak, speak, dread Magian. Tell us what forms were these—of heaven, earth, or hell," exclaimed the king in a dizzy and horror-struck tone, after a moment's profound and awful silence.

"These visions have approved themselves solemn presagings of thy fate. They were no fanciful creations of mine, but were the solemn shadowings of the Infinite," said Raimond, himself much moved. "I adjure thee, O king, as thou now livest on earth, and must live for ever in eternity, repent thus early, forbear from further bloodthirstiness, and save thy ever-living soul from the scorching grasp which, medoubts, is already upon it."

"What says your Grace, will these misty figures turn out aught but an astrologer's mad delusions, or like unto those inspired by the solemnly renewed vigils of a sick man's brain ?" said Sir Ralph Sadler, as he approached and whispered the half-petrified king.

"Ay, truly—by my fay!" cried Henry, shaking off as best he could the unaccountable oppression and the feeling of awe which possessed him. "Such flimsy matter as these ravings of mad chiromancy brooks no thought or belief. Ay, ay, what else is astrology—starry science though it sometimes prove—but a madman's dream and a madman's utterances ?"

"Let the counsel of seventy winters speak. The stars will sooner fall from their ethereal sphere, ere one tittle of the dread drama, but now recited to mortal vision, will fail in coming to pass. 'Tis not often the Eternal, the Great King uncreate, who had no beginning, and will have no end, speaks so awfully to His creatures. Sith the time when the Father of the Faithful of old gazed, by divine command, upwards at the glittering sky of Syria, and was prophesied unto, that his future seed should be as the stars of Heaven for multitude, the Immortal hath but seldom come in direct communion with immortality. The shooting star, which calls away a human life from earth to eternity, vanishes as soon as seen, and leaves naught behind but the silent skies. But why should I make known to thee the mysteries of heaven and its awful condescensions. If thou art an unbeliever in the grace but now offered to thee, than which none more merciful hath been ever aforetime vouchsafed, since the first day-spring shot forth from on high, then, O king, go on thy way, tread the doomed path of deceit, tyranny, cruelty, and blood-guiltiness, weave the web of thy own misery, and meet the fate so awfully foredoomed, the imagination of which however will haunt thee ever, despite thy pride and power, like a fiend—ay, even amid the overpowering mysteries of eternity; while assuredly the brand of history will be prepared to sear thy name through all the generations yet to come."

"Ho, by my faith!—say you so? Then hearken to me, sir wizard, while I prophecy in turn," said the king, with a boisterous albeit forced laugh. "Destiny, I trow, is mightier than all thy spells; and it is not mine to have six yoke-fellows in marriage, however blooming they might prove, or however lusty our years may be. But apart from such unlearned folly, I tell thee I will become so glorious, that my errors—if we have any, of which we are not over certain—shall appear to all men's wondering vision no larger or clearer than the specks on the blazing surface of the mid-day sun, and when our sand of life shall have run out, then shall our name remain as glorious and eternal as that of Solomon or David."

"Peace, peace, O king; there is an impassible barrier between thee and thy visions—ruins and desolation, too, the boldest seers yet dream not of!" retorted Raimond, more in sorrow than in anger. "I wish not to prophesy woes; for are there not enow on earth already? But forasmuch as the patience of Heaven lasts not for ever, and as thou canst not for ever escape the thunder of Jehovah's ire, I, its mouthpiece, bid thee beware. The times themselves are surcharged with the most destructive thunderbolts. They form, even to the searching vision of a Magian's science, a direful phantasmagoria. The hoarse tempest and the volleyed lightning will be brought down from heaven itself, to take part in the dread drama, of which these days form but the evetime. Religion, which hath e'er now broken so many chains, will again be invoked from her starry throne to bear the sword and wave the torch over this chosen land. But the end of all will come, and even thou shalt live to see the wondrous change revolutionizing all things, and in which, alas, thy bloody tyranny will direfully play an active part! But at the last, when thy jocund health shall fail thee, wilt thou have meted out to thee the stern measure so ruthlessly administered by thee unto others. Ere thou diest thou wilt resemble Orestes, who, devising to foil his hideous torments, sought to fly from himself by taking refuge in the grossest de-bauchery; but, in the midst of his orgies, the Furies possessed him, and then, when too late, even death had been most welcome. Bethink thee, O king ! What fate can be foreshadowed more terrible `than thine—to die amid thine own body's living corruption, accursed of God and man, the reproach of all posterity, and the subject of eternal hatred what time the Angel of Wrath shall at last empty his vials upon thee !"

The influence of the weird visions that had been so wondrously revealed had almost lost its late subduing effect; while the words of the astrologer, spoken after so solemn and pro_ phetic a fashion, roused in the heart of the haught tyrant its revengeful throes and more ireful pride. Upon the rest of his auditors, the invocations and prophetic foreshadowings of the Magian produced a powerful and ineffaceable impression. Not so, however, with Henry, who started up, while every limb quivered with rage, his features so inflamed and convulsed, that he more resembled a demoniac than a man under the restraint of reason, and that man. a king.

"It becomes not our Majesty to altercate with madmen and traitors. Wherefore we will leave this one to choke in his own venom," he shouted. "Who knows, but it may perchance be that the chamber hath facilities we wot not of for purposes of mischief!" and he strode with somewhat undignified haste towards the doorway; but he stopped of a sudden on again beholding the sub-prior and his fair penitent, and with a soul ripe for any unjust or vengeful act, he exclaimed, "Fore-gad, sir monk, I mind me of some mischievous plot thou didst venture to predict; we will root it out, and by the saints will set the very nest 'of this accursed faction on fire. I swear by the ashes of holy Peter, I will have all put to the rack—to tortures infinite—till they confess their traitherous schemes. The will of the king sayeth this; and, fore-gad, we'll see if we can't put it in force, despite the lying phenomena of one of Beelzebub's faction. We will, ourselves, preside over a chapter which we appoint ye of Blackfriars to hold on to-morrow's eve after we have partaken of thy monkish hospitality, and feasted amid your good cheer. We will then adjudge this wildfire Maid, and if need be doom her to some striking punishment, for a notable ensample in this cursed coil. I'll warrant me she scapes us not again ! But by my fay, we had well-nigh forgot your penitent, and, methinks, sithence we have changed our will on one matter we may also in another. What say you, son Perrot ?"

" So please you my liege, Mistress More, whose plaintive voice seems to me ever that of Philomela, hath of a surety fastened a spell on my heart, which must irk there for ever," eagerly exclaimed Sir John, standing forward.

" And how inclinest thy heart in this matter, gentle damosel ?" asked Henry of the now newly perturbed Aveline. " Wilt have a root of true English oak for thy mate ?"

" Oh, mock not your woful suppliant, sire !" cried Aveline, as she cast herself on her knees, while trembling beneath this threatened most direful mischance. " I seek no such honour as ye would force on me. My only hope—my every wish—is to fly the world, and throw myself evermore on our Holy Mother's protection."

" O goddess of courtesy and beauty, say not so! I cry you mercy, thou canst not mean to fly the elixirs of life which I can offer thee. Maidens, like moths, are, I well weet, ever attracted by display,," pleaded Sir John Perrot, with great earnestness.

" By St. George, whose garter we wear, we will make a match on it, if only to pleasure thee, son Perrot! We will arrange thy share in it, Mistress More, to thy father's satisfaction. And, to make a long story short, we will ourselves conclude in haste this joyful wedding seeing ye twain in our presence yoked together in the, monastery church to-morrow night, after we have disposed of this womanly wildfire's—the Maid of Kent's—cause. A marriage by torchlight it shall be. See thou to this, sir monk— ordering it in like manner carefully with what we have before entrusted to thy charge," said Henry, with a feeling of vengeful satisfaction.

" This must not—nay, shall not be!" interposed the sub-prior, with a thunderstruck, and yet incredulous look. " If such a sacrilege were attempted, all hell would ring with it some murky midnight."

" Fie—a disturber in canonicals! Go to, sir monk ; this is no matter, I trow, to be wept with tears of blood !" said the king, with a glance of slow, satanic malice at where stood the famed astrologer immersed in some scientific pursuit. " But to favour thee above thy haught brethren as a priest of infinite merit, we decree that thou shalt be the high-priest to solemnize this bridality."

Dan Theodulph forced a contorted smile over his face, though its reflex shadowed back a mental anguish that had never aforetime expressed on human visage so much of its own essence. He tried to speak, but his thoughts careered for the moment so wildly on, they could form no expression, and he remained voiceless, and as one struck dumb.

Aveline More, in misery the most abject, vainly besought of the king a reversal of his tyrannous decision. And even Cromwell, ever more ready to do a kindly act than see a foul one perpetrated, added his interference, concluding with a sentence he bethought might move the stubborn tyrant, that "Damosels were not wont to be thus denied in the times of Carlo Magno, or King Arthur." But nought availed. The flambeau of revengeful passion was burning in his tyrant-heart, as the king seized the arm of Sir John Perrot and moved away from further discussion or beseechance, the while asking his son what he thought of the arch-monk.

"I think him, sire, half Saint, half Satan, and wholly intolerable," replied Sir John Perrot, with mocking significance.

"Attend thou, sir monk, to mine enjoinings. Mark ye, too, that, in or out of reason, we will hold thee responsible for their miscarriage!"

exclaimed the king to the sub-prior, as he passed forth. " Come—let us on, my lords, or the flaming zone of day will catch us in our midnight maraudings."

Then the king and his suite issued forth from the ancient castle, followed more slowly by Dan Theodulph and his despairing penitent.

END OF VOL. II.

London: RICHARD BARRETT, Printer, 13, Mark Lane.